ROYAL BOROUGH OF

Follow us on twitter
Eltham Centre Lib
Archery Road, SE9
Tel: 0203 915 4347
Renewal line: 01527 852384

D1756297

Please return by the last date shown

May 22		

Basu Sharma

Title: BIZUWA: The Lost Tales from the Himalayas

First Edition: May 2021

Author: Basu Sharma

Contact: basushrm@yahoo.co.uk

ISBN: 9798745292040

CHAPTER 1

Exhibition hall!

It was my solo Photo Exhibition in my school. The hall was full of visitors and they were teachers, students, and parents.

Goosebumps! Yes, I could feel Goosebumps on my arms.

The event took off and it was the opening session. The Head Teacher Mr. David Taylor was chairing, and my Class Teacher Mrs. Catherine Jones was mastering the ceremony. There was a banner of the event on the wall behind the Chair and a microphone on a stand at the front of the stage. I was standing in front of the microphone with a guitar – excited, feeling proud but a bit nervous. I gathered all my courage playing with the strings of my guitar for seconds as if I were checking the tunings. Then, I sang a song, which I had practiced, dedicating it to all the young people.

We're the hope
We're the sight
We're the world
We're the light.

It was a stanza of my song. I'd picked the lyrics up from my father's unpublished poetry collection and had composed my own music. I had to make a brief power point presentation about my experiences during my recent holiday trip to Nepal.

Although I had stood and spoken in front of the masses from the stage a couple of times before, when I was a contestant of debate and speech competitions on different occasions, but I had never felt nervousness. But this was something different, neither a competition nor a group presentation. I had to explain everything on my own and answer any question raised during the presentation. For this reason, I thought that I would be self-conscious and would feel nervous. So, I had planned to sing the song at the start to help me overcome the nervousness and build confidence. Playing guitar and singing is my hobby, and I had composed the music. Standing up in front of everyone reminded of me when I had sung this song for my friends in the village during my trip to Nepal.

In the exhibition hall around five hundred photographs were beautifully displayed on the walls. I had taken those photographs myself during my recent one-month long holiday trip to Nepal. Each photograph contained a caption giving a brief description of what it meant. In the middle of the hall there was a nicely decorated table where some beautiful items were displayed, handicrafts of bronze made in my parent's village in Nepal, which I had collected in Nepal as well.

I still remember the speech that my teacher delivered in which she expressed her pride in me; my brief presentation about my travel memoirs; applause after my presentation; visitors observing the photographs and items displayed with much interest and the sale of items in no time; all these scenarios of the exhibition hall were not only exciting but were also very encouraging for me. When the visitors learnt that the exhibition was organised to raise funds to support schools that were in poor condition in the village, it took less than half an hour for everything to be sold. Not only from the sales of the items but also by spontaneous donations of teachers, students and parents in the hall, much more money was raised than had been targeted.

'Perfect! Much better than I'd thought.' I felt a deep satisfaction at how well the exhibition had gone.

But, how could I have had such a grand success with the exhibition on my own? Many had contributed – my teacher, my father and my classmates. All of us worked hard for a week in preparation. We had quite a lot of discussions and rehearsals. For such a grand success of the exhibition, the credit goes mostly to my teacher and my father.

When I returned to my school from the vacation and shared my idea of organising a photo exhibition in the school, my teacher was happier than me. She put her hand on my shoulder and said, 'Excellent idea, Robin, go ahead'.

Then she instantly took on the responsibility to make it happen. She took the lead role in planning and organising, what and how to display and whom to invite. She provided me with a continuous guidance until the exhibition took place successfully.

My father helped me select photographs for the exhibition, printed them off and prepared my power point presentation. My classmates' contributions were no less. They not only extended their helping hands during my preparation but also their questions and curiosity helped me a lot while selecting materials and preparing for the explanations during my presentation.

Finally, my grandma's stories and her blessings were always with me, although she was thousands of miles away in the village, guiding me in every moment while I prepared the slides for my presentation. Likewise, I would not have been able to collect photographs and other items to display in the exhibition without the help of my friends in the village during my visit.

In fact, the contributions from all of them was the key to the success of my exhibition. I thanked them all from the bottom of my heart.

My dad and mom had also attended the event and when we came back home dad and I started reviewing the exhibition. Mom joined us later after Greta, my little sister, came home from school.

'How are you feeling now, Robin?' Dad asked.

'I'm so happy. I can't even express it in words.' I replied.

'So, this vacation was a nice one then?'

'Not just nice, it was terrific' I said. 'In the end, the exhibition was organised in such a fantastic way. It made me miss Nepal. The natural beauty is like heaven on earth. Everything you told me about Nepal was true! Grandma's stories were invaluable gifts too. I can't wait to go back'.

While we were talking, mom got the dinner ready. I took my dinner, and I went to my bedroom. I went to bed and recalled moments from my holiday. Right from the beginning when the holiday was planned to every day in the month I had spent in the village. Scene after scene it all came back to me like a movie in my mind.

CHAPTER 2

I was happy because my dreams had come true. My little sister Greta and I, along with my dad and mom, were travelling to Nepal. Greta was just a seven-year old girl. She could not understand much about this trip. But, I could. I was fifteen-year old. I was feeling so good about the trip. I had been waiting for it to be morning since last night, I could not sleep properly due to the excitement.

'Robin, get dressed and come quickly for breakfast; I could hear my mom yelling from my room. 'We will soon leave for the airport' – mom was bringing breakfast. I quickly went to the washroom and got ready to join mom, dad and Greta at the breakfast table. We had all our luggage ready by last night. Shortly after our breakfast we were on our way to Heathrow airport.

I knew that we had our family home in a hilly village of Nepal called *Chainpur*. Dad was born there, a village on the lap of Mt. Makalu in eastern Nepal. I have heard many times from him about the natural beauty of

Chainpur which had made me rather impatient to be there.

This was my first trip to Nepal. I had travelled abroad across Europe but never got a chance to go to Nepal. Dad used to go alone to see my grandma every year. This time we were all going there together. Last year when my dad went to see my grandma, she insisted he takes us when he would come to visit her next.

'Thanks grandma, I will see you soon!', I thanked her but unexpressed.

Dad and mom had told me many times about Nepal, our village and my grandma. But I had never seen them myself. This time I had a chance to see for myself. This made me extremely excited. I had told my school friends about my trip and I also to my teacher. My teacher was happy to know that I was visiting my village and my grandma.

'Robin, I should give you a project then'. My teacher told me. She advised me, 'Make notes of where you travel, what you see, what you hear and what you experience. If possible, bring some relevant photographs, too. Upon your return, you could make a presentation. Will you do it, Robin?'

'Yes, ma'am, I'll do it' – I had replied. When I came back home after school, I told my dad about the project I had been given and asked him to buy a camera for me. The next day, when he came back from work, he had brought a nice slim camera. I had already put a notebook and a pen in my bag and now the camera.

At Heathrow airport, while waiting to board the plane, I was remembering my classmates; especially, I remembered Philip. Last year, he had gone to Peterborough on holiday to see his grandparents. He stayed there for two weeks with them. I still remember what he told me about his trip. He was so excited to tell the stories his grandma had told him. This time, I was going to see my grandma, too.

'I'll be with my grandma for four weeks and she will tell me loads of stories. Then, I can also tell my friends those stories. Especially, I'll be very happy to tell Philip' – I was lost in my own imagination.

We boarded the plane. The plane flew higher and higher in the sky. I had taken a seat by the window. I took photos of the views with my new camera.

CHAPTER 3

Kathmandu – the capital city of Nepal.

We arrived in Kathmandu in the morning flying from London the previous day. Dad had planned to stay in Kathmandu that day and the following day to sightsee and then go to the village. *Pashupatinath*, *Swayambhunath*, *Basantpur Durbar* Square, *Hanumandhoka*, *Patan Durbar* Square and *Bhaktapur Nyahtapol* were a few places where dad had said he would take me. I had jotted down these names in my notebook.

But dad's plan fell through. While coming out of the airport, we learnt that there was a Kathmandu valley wide closure for an uncertain time. At the immigration desk, I could hear an immigration officer mentioning about such a closure.

'What does this valley wide closure mean, dad?' I asked.

'Valley wide closure means a general strike in the Kathmandu valley. Schools, colleges, transportation, markets, factories, they are all closed. Today, we have to reach our hotel by walking. Taxis, buses nothing will be available.' I felt frustrated.

'It is so annoying! I already felt queasy from jetlag. And, now I had to walk to the hotel. How far would our hotel be?' I was annoyed.

We started walking down from the airport. Dad was pulling two suitcases. My sister was holding mom's hand and walking with her. I was carrying my bag on my back and walked along. There were people walking on the road. There were no vehicles on the street. I saw only two people on bicycles.

'Who has caused everything to be closed? Why are they doing this? This doesn't happen in London. Bus strikes are only for a couple of days. Even if there is a bus strike, cabs and other vehicles still run', I muttered this under my breath.

When we reached the ring road down from the airport, we saw a motorcycle on fire. Dad asked the people walking on the road and one of them replied, 'a farmer from a village called *Gothatar* was carrying two drums of milk to take to his customers. A group of youths, closure cadres, stopped him and burnt his motorbike'. The milk was spilled all over the ground, the empty drums were lying further away, and the motorbike was already half burnt.

Although I felt terrible that such a thing had happened, I wanted to include this memory in my project presentation. So, I took my camera out and began taking photographs.

'Who will compensate that poor farmer? Will those nasty youths and their leaders be punished or not? Whoever they are, they are criminals to do such nasty deeds.' I questioned and gave my verdict to myself but unexpressed.

We walked ahead. There were motor tyres burning on the road. Black smoke was rising high in the sky polluting the atmosphere. Stones and bricks were piled up to block the road. We observed many more similar scenes until we reached our hotel. All of these were done by those closure supporters. There was a group of youths at a point on our way to the hotel and they were the cadres of the strikers. I could read signs of victory on their faces. We continued walking non-stop observing all those scenes and reached our hotel an hour later. Thank God, the hotel was not that far.

CHAPTER 4

At the hotel, my sister Greta and I went straight to bed. When I woke up, my mother told me that I had slept deeply for almost three hours.

'Go and get washed. We will have our lunch, now.' Mom said. Greta had got up half an hour earlier and mom had got her to take a shower. Dad and mom had also freshened up already.

Soon after, we were at the dining table in the hotel and were having our lunch. While having lunch, dad raised issues about our plan to visit different places in Kathmandu. 'We have to change our plan of visiting different places because of the strike situation. But, the plan for today to go to my friend Satyandra is unchanged. It will only take fifteen minutes to reach his house walking from our hotel. You're not feeling tired anymore, son, are you?'

I nodded my head and said, 'I'm not feeling tired anymore'.

'This place where we are staying now is called *Battisputali*. Satyandra's house is in the place called *Sifal*.' Dad explained our further plans, 'We will go to see them today and will have dinner with them. Tomorrow morning, we will visit the *Pashupatinath* and *Guhyesgwori* temples. Unfortunately, we won't be able to visit *Basantapur Durbar* Square, *Patan Durbar* Square, *Bhaktaput Nyhtapol* and *Swayambhunath* this time. They are all in distant places and we can't go without taxis. So, we will visit those places after we return from the village if possible. However, we will go tomorrow after *Pashupatinath* and *Guhyeshwori* temples to *Bouddhanath* monastery, which is a sacred *Buddhist* shrine like *Swayambhunath* and we can go there by walking. Is that alright, my boy?'

'Alright.' I answered him but I was not feeling so happy. I had heard about all those other places from dad and mom and was keen to visit. 'What will happen after returning from the village, not sure. There may still be a strike on.' I had my doubts but did not express them.

After lunch, we went to our room and got ready to go to uncle Satyandra's house. Mom packed the gifts, which she had brought from London, for uncle Satyandra's son and daughter. Around four o'clock in the afternoon, we set out from the hotel and reached there after a walk of about fifteen minutes.

I had met already uncle Satyandra. Last year, he had come to our house in London. He was a nice man, very friendly. He had long chats with me. He had told me quite a lot about Nepal, especially the people, culture and traditions and the natural beauties. He had told me interesting stories, so, I could still remember.

I also found his wife, aunty Ganga, to be a nice lady. She was expressive with a smiling face and was very friendly. Their children were still small kids. Their son Naresh was as big as my sister Greta, seven years old, and their daughter Nabina a child of three years. Greta and Naresh started playing video games in a corner. I joined dad, mom, uncle and aunty in their conversation.

It was nice to learn that aunty Ganga used to paint as her hobby. She had many paintings. She brought around ten and showed them to us. She had used water colour for all her paintings. She gave me a beautiful painting of Mt. Everest as a gift.

'What a beautiful painting!' I thanked her.

'Would you prefer Nepalese dishes, Om?' Uncle Satyandra asked my dad.

'Yes, that would be great. We make Nepalese meals in London, too, from time to time'. My mom replied instead of dad.

'So, that's sorted. We have today prepared a Nepalese meal. We will have starter with typically *Newari* items – *Choyala*, *Sandeko Bhatmas*, *Chiura*, *Aluko Tarkari* and *Masko Bara* (roasted meat with spices, roasted soyabean with spices, beaten rice, potato fried curry and black lentil bread) and, of course, home-made spirit. How does that sound, Laxmi?' Now it was aunty Ganga who asked mom.

'Wonderful! A long-awaited wish will be fulfilled,' was mom's reaction.

Uncle Satyandra and aunty Ganga belonged to a Nepalese ethnic group called *Newar.* So, it was obvious that they had offered *Newari* menu as starters in the dinner. *Newari* cuisine is immensely popular not only within the *Newar* community but among all the Nepalese people.

Their conversation revolved around many subjects. They talked about our schools and education. They also talked quite a lot about politics in Nepal. They were saying 'if it continues to happen, our country will be totally ruined'. I did not understand much about those political issues. I just listened to them, quietly. The home-made spirit was adding a glow to their conversation. We, the children, were enjoying our snacks with the orange squash aunty Ganga had made herself.

An Interesting chat was going on while we were enjoying the snacks and drinks, when suddenly the electricity was cut, and the room turned dark. However, uncle and aunty were aware that there would be a power cut. Uncle Satyandra lit a candle and said, 'Look Om, our situation. We are rich in hydropower, but it is our destiny to live in darkness. But, don't worry. I've got an inverter to cope with such a load shading. Let me quickly go to the next room to put the lights back.'

Then he went to the next room, put the lights back and came in. Load shading and inverters were new things to me. I asked him, 'Uncle, what is a load shading and an inverter?'

'A load shading is a planned power cut. These days, we have load shading of ten hours every day. It is ridiculous that there is a power cut when we need power the most. So, we have arranged an inverter to have lights on during the load shading time. An inverter is a power generator which is rechargeable. We recharge the inverter while there is power and use it when we need it. Was my answer for you clear, dear boy?' Uncle Satyandra asked me.

'Yeah. I'm clear now,' I replied.

Thank God, they had an inverter, and we did not have to stay only in candle lights. I never knew about such a load shading. I had never experienced it in London.

We returned to the hotel in the late evening after having dinner. The streets were dark as well due to the load shading. Uncle Satyandra escorted us to our hotel with a torch in his hand. I had to wake up early in the morning to go to the *Pashupatinath* and *Guhyeswari* temples and *Bouddhanath* monastery. So, I changed quickly and went straight to bed.

CHAPTER 5

All four of us set out for the *Pashupatinath* temple. While walking from a junction called *Gaushala* to the temple, I felt excitement, curiosity, fear and disappointment one after another. Green forest adjoining the street, monkeys coming out from the forest on to the street and a crowd of people walking to and from the *Pashupatinath* temple were nice to see. I was scared to see the monkeys trying to snatch things that people were carrying. but I felt safe to be with dad and mom.

Meanwhile, I was very saddened to see elderly people and children sitting on both sides of the streets begging. Why are they begging? Isn't there anyone to look after them? Not even the government? Do these beggar children go to school? These questions swirled around in my mind. My father may not have answers to these questions either.

Despite feeling sad about the poverty, I saw, the artistic pagoda style model of the *Pashupatinath* temple was still a great attraction, and a charming and a divinely place. I was eager to know when and by who this temple was built. I asked my dad.

'I'll tell you the history when we go back to the hotel, It's a bit long.' He replied.

I had a nice view of everything in and around the *Pashupatinath* temple complex. There were shops of statuettes, ornaments, and worshipping stuff on one side of the street being the opposite side the temple compound. In every shop, there was massively displayed *Rudrakshamala* (garlands of a kind of seeds). I asked dad to tell me about the importance of *Rudraksha.* Although I'd little knowledge that it is regarded as sacred thing in Hindu religion, I wanted to

learn more when I saw that bulk. Then he described, 'It is the seed of a typical mountain plant species of *Elaeocarpus Ganitrus* which has no common English name. This seed is used traditionally by *Hindus* as prayer beads. The name *Rudraksha* comes from *Sanskrit* language and is derived from the combination of two words *Rudra* and *Aksha*. *Rudra* is Lord *Shiva's* another name and *Aksha* means tear drop in *Sanskrit*. So, *Rudraksha* means Lord *Shiva's* teardrops. Since, it is associated with Lord *Shiva,* it is regarded as a sacred seed and people have been using it traditionally as prayer beads in Hindu religion'.

'But you know my son,' He continued describing about *Rudraksha,* 'It has become equally popular among

Buddhists, too. There is a high demand of *Rudraksha* these days and Nepal exports it to India and China every year worth of millions of Rupees. Before, people used to rely on the natural production of it but now, because of the increased demand, farmers have started planting it in their farmlands. This species is found only in the mountain region, mainly in Nepal and more specifically in the region where there is our village. I have heard that famers are making thousands of Rupees from a single tree. Hence, it is now a good attraction for the farmers of the region to grow it in their farmlands.'

It was nice to learn about the importance and the growing business of *Rudraksha.* Mom had to buy worshipping stuff. She went to a shop where an elderly woman had a stall. She bought a tray full of different items. The tray was home made of *Sal* tree leaves. It was made so artistically that the *Sal* tree leaves were stitched in two layers with bamboo needles to make the tray. Mom said that the *Sal* tree leaf plates are used traditionally for worshipping and in the feasts, too, as dinner plates in the villages. The items in the tray were flowers, red and yellow powders, two pieces of red and white cloths, wood apple tree leaves and a dry whole coconut ball but unhusked. Dad did not forget to tell me that the wood apple leaf which is called *Belpatra* in local language is a must for worshipping Lord *Shiva*. Mom topped up the tray buying some fruits separately.

After mom grabbed the tray of worshipping items, we walked ahead and reached the main entrance of the temple. There were two signs displayed at the entrance. One sign had informed the devotees that the shoes and the leather goods were not allowed inside the gate. There were locker rooms on both sides of the gate. Dad hired a locker and we put off and stored our shoes, leather belts and leather bags there. The other sign was about the restriction of entrance for other than Hindus and said that only Hindus could enter. I didn't understand why non-Hindus were restricted. What would they harm to the temple? Surely, they could learn something about the Hindu beliefs. I'm a Hindu by birth but I've been to churches in London and there is no such restriction for the non-Christians. I had some questions and opinions after reading that sign but did not express them.

We entered through the main gate and there were steps to walk down to the temple yard. I'd had a nice front view of the temple. I wanted to have a glimpse and stood on the top landing of the steps to look around. My eyes and mind were full of the pagoda style structure of the main temple, nicely carved rafters, a big copper sculpture of a bullock on the front yard of the temple, a long queue of the devotees, et cetera. There were monkeys on the ground and on the roofs. It was nice to see the monkey troops jumping from one roof to another, from roof to the ground and climbing up to the roofs, some carrying their babies cuddled. It was fun to watch a large flight of pigeons competing to eat rice grains in the yard that had been spread by devotees.

I walked down to the spot where there was the pigeon flock. I wanted to be with them. But, when I approached, all of them flew off. When they flew off, I felt a mild and melodious sound and a pleasant breeze produced by their wings. What a wonderful feeling of peace I had in my mind! I closed my eyes and took a breath of that breeze.

The main temple of *Pashupatinath,* which is built in Nepalese *Pagoda* style, has two levelled roofs of copper with gold covering. It has silver covered four main doors. The *Pagoda* style structure is that the temple is built on a square shape from the base platform up to the base of the first level of roof. Then, all four sides of the roof are made slope to make it narrower on the top. The second level of the roof is made on the top of the first level which has again all its four sides sloped to make the pinnacle of the temple pointed. The temple's pinnacle is called *Gazur* in the local language and this *Gazur* is also gold covered.

When reached the temple, we made three circles of the temple by walking clockwise and then lined up in the queue of the devotees. Moving slowly in the queue, we reached the west door of the temple. My mother was carrying the tray of worshipping items she bought a while ago to offer to Lord *Shiva.* There was a big *Shivlinga* (Lord *Shiva's* figurine), black coloured, inside the temple in the middle of the floor. There were priests, one main priest and his assistants, around the *Shivlinga.* All priests had long tufts of hair on top of their shaven heads. They had *Janai* (the holy thread) worn cross from left shoulder to beneath the right armpit under the right hand. They had worn maroon-coloured *Dhotis.* A *Dhoti* is an unsewn piece of cloth generally used by priests as their traditional costume. One of the assisting priests came to the door, poured a little holy water on our palms each, which we drank. He took the tray from my mom and offered it to Lord *Shiva* placing the items on the platform of *Shivlinga*. He broke the coconut ball smashing it on the floor and offered the coconut water to *Shivlinga*. Then he returned the tray putting back on it some pieces of flower, pieces of red and white coloured cloth, a piece of broken coconut, a banana and a little sandalwood paste.

After finishing worshipping, we visited every corner of the temple while my dad described different aspects of the temple. 'This temple complex is one of the UNESCO World Heritage Sites. There is always crowd of devotees and worshippers in the temple. But the main festival observed in this shrine is called *Mahashivaratri,* the day dedicated to Lord *Shiva,* which falls in the month of March. It is estimated that around a million devotees visit here every year on the day of festival. There are more than five hundred temples and monuments and 184 *Shivlingas* (figurines of Lord *Shiva*) in the complex.'

We headed towards the *Guhyeswari* temple. We walked down to the River *Bagmati* at the back of the *Pashupatinath* temple and crossed the river through a bridge over it. There were beautifully paved stone steps to climb up to the hill. The stone paved trail ran through a forest. We walked along the steps up to the top of the hill and down to the temple. *Guhyeshwori* is one of the famous *Shaktipithas* (shrines of the almighty Goddess). There were similar scenes of a queue of devotees, flights of pigeons and the monkey troops. Shoes and leather goods were not allowed into this temple, too, so we took these off in a corner and lined up in the queue. We had to wait for about fifteen minutes to enter the temple to worship.

After the *Guhyeshwori* temple, we went to *Bouddhnath Stupa* (one of the main Buddhist monasteries in Nepal). It took around half an hour to reach there walking through narrow streets.

It was a huge mound-shaped *Stupa* (monastery) having its

pinnacle in three levels with three different shapes. The bottom part of the pinnacle was square shaped and there were watchful eyes of Lord *Buddha* painted on all four sides. The middle part of the pinnacle was a masonry work but gradually narrowing upward like a pyramid and the apex was a metallic object with an umbrella shape ending by a pointed object. There were spinning prayer wheels around the base of the dome which were carved with sacred Buddhist mantras and there were colourful prayer flags strung all around the giant mandala. Seeing those eyes, prayer wheels and flags, I felt a deep peace in my mind, it was a strange feeling. I realised then why Lord *Buddha* is said to be a God of Peace. There was a crowd of pilgrims including Buddhist Monks in maroon robes and shaven heads who were making a circle of the dome spinning the prayer wheels. Like in the temples of *Pashupatinath* and *Guhyeshwari* earlier, there were monkey troops and pigeon flights all around the *Stupa*.

I enjoyed the *Stupa* and felt at peace there. I was eager to know about the story of *Bouddhanath* temple and expressed my interest to my dad. He told me that the *Stupa* is the holiest Tibetan Buddhist temple outside Tibet, and he promised that he would tell me the full story back at our hotel. I took in the scenery with my eyes and took more photos with my camera.

CHAPTER 6

When we were back to our hotel, it was already one o'clock in the afternoon. We were late for our lunch and I was feeling hungry. So, we quickly had our lunch.

The first thing I asked dad was to tell me about the *Pashupatinath* temple when we were in our room after our lunch.

'I may not be able to tell everything about the story of *Pashupatinath* temple. However, I'll tell you what I know. I think you should make notes which may be useful for your presentation of your project. So, get ready with your notebook and pen, my boy.' Dad gave me time to get ready instead of starting to tell me the story straightaway.

My pen was poised!

'There is no historical evidence yet whatsoever of when the temple was first built.' Dad started the story. 'Most of the beliefs are based on folklores. However, the first written evidence of the existence of the *Pashupatinath* temple is found since 400 AD. There weren't the same structures of the temple and its surroundings then that we have today. According to the available historical evidence, the previous temple was destroyed by termites and the present pagoda style structure of the main temple was built by King *Shupushpa* of the *Lichchhavi* dynasty in the 15th century. Since then, there have been built many small or big structures on both sides of the river. Improvement works took place and the temple and its surroundings have been developed to the present form. The *Guhyeswari* temple was built before king *Shupushpa* in the 11th century.' said Dad. I took notes in my notebook.

'These are the historical facts that I know. There are many legends and people's beliefs about the *Pahupatinath* temple. Among them, I'm telling you the most famous one.' Having said this, dad paused for a while. I was listening to him intently. Mom was also listening to him attentively. My sister was sitting by mom and she was playing video games on the iPad. When dad paused, we could hear a pin drop.

Dad broke the silence and continued telling me the story – 'According to the legend, long ago in the

prehistoric time called *Satyayug* Lord *Shiva* suddenly disappeared from his residence in the Himalayas. He took the form of a deer and started wandering unknown in the thick forest called *Shleshmantak* to the east bank of the *Bagmati* river. His wife Goddess *Parvati* was worried when she did not see him in their residence. She looked around for him and when she could not find him, she asked other Gods to find and bring him back.'

'All of the Gods took the matter seriously and started looking for him. There would be an adverse situation in managing the universe if there would be no Lord *Shiva* in his place, who is also regarded as the God of Gods. Finally, they spotted him in the *Shleshmantak* forest in the form of a deer. They asked him to leave his deer form and return to his residence in his real form. He did not listen to them even when they said that Goddess *Parvati* was very worried. Then the Gods decided to catch him forcefully and take him back. The Gods made efforts collectively to catch the deer. The deer ran away from them and crossed the river. The Gods, too, chased him and finally were able to catch him by his horn. There was a forceful tug-of-war between the deer and the Gods. Because of which a piece of the deer's antlers (horn) broke and fell down on the earth.'

Dad was telling me the story in an interesting way and I was listening to him attentively. I was imagining the tug-of-war between the deer and the Gods. Dad continued, 'The Gods worshiped the broken piece of the horn as a figurine of Lord *Shiva* and prayed to him. With the Gods' prayers, Lord *Shiva* was pleased, gave up the deer's form, appeared in his real form and blessed them. Lord *Shiva* then returned home in the Himalayas and lived with Goddess *Parvati* as usual. At the spot where the broken piece of horn of the deer had fallen, there is now *Pashupatinath*'s *Shivlinga* which is widely known as *Jyotirlinga*.

I stopped dad's flow and asked, 'Dad, I got a bit lost with the broken piece of deer's horn, *Shivlinga* and

Jyotirlinga. Before you take the story further, will you please explain to me what difference is between *Shivlinga* and *Jyotirlinga*? If I have to describe a *Shivlinga* and a *Jyotirlinga* to my friends upon returning to London to help them understand clearly what they are, how can I better describe them? Also, will you please clarify for me if a piece of the horn of every deer is regarded as a *Shivlinga* or not'?

'Sure, I will. At the same time, I would recommend that you take help of a picture of the *Shivlinga*, too. Don't get confused with the broken piece of the deer's horn, it was just that one occasion when the Gods regarded it as a figurine of Lord *Shiva* and worshipped only because it was the piece of the horn of that particular deer which Lord *Shiva* had taken the form of.'

'Now, let me describe a *Shivlinga* in short. It is a figurine or statuette of Lord *Shiva*. Unlike the statues of other Gods, normally there is no figure of Lord *Shiva* on it. It's a solid object, made up mainly of stone, which is cylinder shaped with its one end attached to a circle shaped flat base and the other end rounded. The base at one point on its circumference is pointed like an arrow. The *Shivlinga* is placed upright on its base in such a way that the arrow of its base points towards North. You will find a *Shivlinga* in every shrine of Lord *Shiva*. Not all *Shivlingas* are called *Jyotirlingas*. In particular, the *Shivlinga* which is in the temple of *Pashupatinath* is called *Jyotirlinga,* and, I think, there are only one or two more *Jyotirlingas*. I'll explain the reason why this one is called *Jtyotirlinga* in the story ahead. Defining simply a *Jyotirlinga*, it's a *Shivlinga* that

shines or flashes or throws lights.'

'Why is the arrow of the *Shivlinga's* base pointing towards North?'

'You know that Lord *Shiva* is a Hindu God and the region where the *Hindu* religion originated is to the south from the Himalayas. I mentioned earlier that the Himalaya is the residence of Lord *Shiva*, which is towards the North from the region where *Hindus* live. Perhaps, people of this region initially placed the *Shivlinga* with the arrow on its base pointing towards North simply to indicate the residence of Lord *Shiva* and the tradition continued until today, not only in this region but everywhere now.'

'I understand now, thanks dad'.

He continued, 'You should remember that there was a tug-of-war between the deer form of Lord *Shiva* and other Gods, a piece of horn of the deer was broken and dropped on earth and the Gods worshipped it as Lord *Shiva's* figurine and prayed to him. Over time, the deer's broken piece of horn became buried in the soil and disappeared. People did not know about it. After many centuries, a cow herder discovered a shining *Shivlinga* at the same spot where the piece of horn was buried. The story is interesting.'

According to the legend, there was a big grazing field for the cattle around *Pashupatinath*'s temple. The grazing field covered from where the airport is today to *Battisputali* where the hotel we are staying is. Every day, herdsmen used to bring hundreds of their cattle for grazing in this field.

Then, an incredible incident happened one day. It had been few days; one cow of a herdsman had stopped milking in the evening after coming back from the grazing field. He suspected that someone might have milked his cow in the grazing field. He decided to find out the truth. On the day, the incident happened, he followed his cow. Wherever his cow went, he followed her but silently and hiding himself. In the end, what he

saw made his eyes bulge open. Nobody had milked his cow in the grazing field. Instead, his cow went straight to the place where the piece of deer's horn was buried and where today there is a *Shivlinga* and started showering her milk on the earth. Seeing such an unbelievable scene, the herdsman called all other herdsmen and showed the spot which was still wet with the cow's milk. They called the local people and explained what happened. Such an incident surprised everyone.

The local people became curious to know why the cow did that and they decided to dig up the place to find out the reason. They started digging the land very carefully. After digging around three meters deep, the top end of the *Shivlinga* appeared which was flashing light. The flashing light dazzled them, and they could not look at it continuously. But, after a while, the flashing light gradually started dimming and stopped in the end. When the flashing light stopped completely, they again continued digging at the periphery of the *Shivlinga* and brought the whole *Shivlinga* up to ground level and made it stable. Because it flashed light while coming over ground, people gave it the name as *Jyotirlinga*, that means flashing *Shivlinga*.

Then the local people built a temple with walls around the *Shivlinga* in a few days' time. They called the temple *Pashupatinath*. They arranged for a priest to offer the God a regular worship, twice a day, early in the morning and in the evening. It is believed that the *Shivlinga* used to flash light for many years twice a day, early in the morning and in the evening. The twice daily worshiping was started following the *Shivlinga* flashing light in the morning and in the evening. The tradition of worshiping twice daily continues today.

Dad finished the story and said, 'There are some other myths about the *Pashupatinath* temple, but they are not very much different from this story. So, let's complete this story here. Okay, my son?'

'Okay', I replied but was still lost within the story. What an interesting story! I had listened with much interest, and now I recalled the main points and noted them down in my notebook. Dad kept quiet until I finished taking my notes and looked at him.

CHAPTER 7

I finished taking all my notes about the story of the temple of *Pashupatinath* and was ready to listen to my dad ahead. I looked at him and asked him to proceed. Then he jumped to the story of *Bouddhanath* temple.

'As I told you earlier, *Bouddhanath* temple is a Tibetan Biddhist temple outside Tibet. Like the temple of *Pashupatinath,* it is also one of the UNESCO World Heritage Sites. As you saw this morning a crowd of people, thousands of pilgrims come here every day to make a *Kora* spinning the prayer wheels. A *Kora* means a ritual circumnavigation of the *Stupa* in local language. You might have seen when they make a circle, they also spin the prayer wheels. You might have also noticed letters printed on the spinning wheels and they are the mantras. Did you see the Buddhist monks in maroon robes and with shaven heads having carried prayer bead strings in their hands? They chant mantras very softly and use the beads for prayer. Did you see the colourful prayer flags strung all around the *Stupa,* my son?'

'Yes, I did. I loved them.' I replied.

'Images and mantras are printed on those flags. Buddhists believe that those prayer flags with images and mantras have immense spiritual power and when air passes through them, the air will then flow carrying energy, kindness and blessings of God for the people.

Now, let me tell you the stories about *Bouddhanath*. There are mainly two legends. One is a local legend and the other one a Tibetan. Both stories are not very much different to each other. Both have the same characters, a mother and her four sons, who built the *Bouddhanath Stupa.* And, both legends are linked to Tibet.

According to the local legend, long ago, an *Apsara* was cursed by gods for her reduced spiritual merit and had to take birth on earth in an ordinary family. An *Apsara* is a celestial nymph or maiden or a beautiful supernatural female being or mainly known as a beautiful female dancer in the heaven. She was known as *Majyajima* in her new life. She had four husbands and she had four sons, one from each husband. Her sons were known as *Tajibu, Phagjibu, Khyijibu* and

Jyajibu. They all were followers of Buddhism. They decided to build a *Stupa* and soon started its construction. They carried the construction materials (soil, bricks and stones) on elephant, horses and donkeys. *Majyajima* died before it was completed but her sons continued and completed it.

After completion of the *Stupa* construction, *Lamas* (Buddhist Monks) came and prayed to God to reside here. By their prayers and mantras, the rays of *Bodhisattvas* (Buddhahood) reached the heaven and a holy sound was heard in the sky and, because the *Stupa* was empowered by *Bodhisattvas,* Buddha incarnated as *Lamas* (Buddhist Gurus or Monks) in *Bauddhanath.* The four sons of *Majyajima* wished to disseminate Buddhism and after the completion of the construction of the *Stupa,* they prayed for their next lives for this cause. Because of their devout and prayers, they were reborn in Tibet as Kings, Administrators and Enlightened Gurus.

Tibetan mythology does not mention about the mother being a cursed nymph. It says that an old woman with her four sons built a huge mound on the grave of a great saint known as *Kasyapa Buddha* who lived long before *Gautam Buddha.* For this and further construction, the old woman asked for a permission from the then King of the City. The king gave his permission, but his ministers and officers did not like such a massive construction and asked the king to cancel or withdraw his decision. But the king dismissed his ministers' request as an inappropriate and he said that a king cannot withdraw his decision once taken. So, the construction of the *Stupa* was finished with the order of his permission.

There is a long list of what *Majyajima's* four sons did in protecting the religion and disseminating Buddhism as powerful persons in their next lives. I am not taking you that side of the story now. Instead, I will tell you a tale about the importance of making circles of the holy *Stupa.*

According to the story, there was a shop owner. He was a greedy, characterless, and sulky man and one who did not follow social and religious norms. He had committed many sinful acts in his life. For such sinful acts, he fell to hell when he died. He was sentenced to hard punishment by the King of the hell. When the King of the hell was about to execute his punishment, Lord

Buddha appeared and nullified his punishment. The King and all the administrators of the hell were surprised and asked Lord *Buddha* why his punishment was nullified. Buddha said that although the man had committed many sins in his life, he had once made a full circle of the holy *Bouddhanath Stupa* while he was chasing a dog and, hence, had earned a religious merit to be rewarded for. As a reward for his even a single religious merit he had gained, he would be given a chance to correct himself. The man realised his sins, prayed to Lord *Buddha* and begged for a chance that he would do all his best to atone himself with religious acts in his next life. The man became a Buddhist Monk in his next life and spent all his life in *Bouddhanath* and was actively involved in disseminating Buddhism. This is a myth about the importance of *Bouddhanath.'*

'How did you find it, Robin?'

'Interesting! I liked it very much.' I replied.

'Great! Now, let me tell you some bits of the historical records about the *Bouddhanath Stupa.* According to *Gopalbansawali,* one of the ancient Nepalese chronicles, the then *Lichchhavi* King of Nepal *Shivdev* had built the *Stupa* towards the end of 6th century of the Christian Era. However, other chronicles are found to date it a century ago towards the end of 5th century during the King *Mandev's* regime. The Tibetan source states that the bones of King *Amshuverma,* who ruled between 605-621 AD, were found when the mound was excavated later towards the end of 15th or start of 16th centuries. Likewise, the Tibetan King *Trisong Detsan,* who lived between 755-797 AD, is also said to be associated with the construction of the *Stupa.'*

'Looking at these dates', he concluded the story, 'It is clear that the *Bouddhanath Stupa* was built after almost one thousand years of Lord *Buddha's* demise. This is all what I know about its construction and, I think, this is enough to you, too, for now. Ok, my son?'

'Ok.'

'Then take your notes. I'll wait for you.'

CHAPTER 8

My dad was waiting for me. When I looked at him, he spoke, 'Robin, I think you found the stories interesting. Now, I'll tell you one more story, which is interesting as well. This story is related to *Battisputali*, the name of the place where the hotel we are staying in now is located. The story is all about why the name of this place was given to be *Battisputali* (thirty-two butterflies).'

I was extremely interested in hearing what the story was all about.

'If you tell all of the stories at once, how can he remember them all? The stories will be mixed up and overlap with one another.' My mom said. She had been listening with me all this time. I was irritated. I wanted more stories!

'How could they overlap mum? Every day I have different lessons on different subjects at school. Don't worry mom, it won't overlap. Tell me the story, dad. I'm eager to hear more.' I said.

'The folklore about why the name of this place was given to be *Battisputali* is really interesting. Do you remember? I had told you in the previous story that there was a large grazing field from the place where the airport is today to the place where we are staying now, where everyday hundreds of herdsmen used to bring their cattle for grazing.'

'Yes, I do.' I replied.

According to the legend, there was a small, beautiful hill on the part of the grazing field where *Battisputali* is now. On the top of the hill, there was a piece of flat shining stone. Every day the herdsmen used to leave their cattle to graze in the field and they used to gather at the bottom of the hill. They had made a marking line there. Then they used to have a race from the marking line to the top of the hill. Whoever could reach the shining stone on the top first, he used to become their King for the whole day. The second runner as minister and then all others his forces for the day. The King of the herdsmen used to rule there for that day. Everyone used to obey the king's order. The king used to give order from time to time to his minister and the force men to monitor their cattle's situation, report to him and keep the cattle in the field in order. His orders used to be obeyed by all. As if they were running the state's administration system perfectly.

There was a pedestrian track a bit away from the hill. One day, the herdsman King seated on his throne stone saw four people walking along that pedestrian track. There were three men and a woman. The woman was behind all the men and the King saw her crying. The King thought they might be in trouble and ordered his minister and force men to bring them in front of him. Following the King's order, his men went to them, arrested them and brought them in front of the King. The King questioned the woman why she was crying. Then the woman told her sorrowful story.

'What had happened to them, dad?' I asked him because he had paused again.

'Stay patient, my son. I'll tell you the full story.'

Among the three men, one was the woman's husband and the other two were villagers. The woman's husband and one of the other two villagers had gone abroad together for work two years earlier. The woman's husband had worked hard and earned good money. He had saved every penny possible. After a year, the other villager returned home. The woman's husband had sent his savings home to his wife with the man. Instead of sending all the cash, he decided to send a little cash and with the rest of his money he bought and sent a piece of diamond. The man gave the little cash to his wife but did not give her the piece of diamond.

After a year, he also returned home. Upon returning home, he asked his wife to bring that piece of diamond. The woman did not know about the diamond and was shocked. She asked her husband which piece of diamond he was talking about. Then he told her that he had sent some cash and a piece of diamond with the villager. She told him that the villager did not give any piece of diamond, but a little cash and she did not know about the diamond. Hearing his wife, the man felt like dropping to the ground. Immediately, he went to the villager's house and asked for the diamond. The villager told a different story. He told that he had given both the cash and the piece of diamond to his wife immediately after he came back to the village. He even presented one of his neighbours as his witness who, he told, was together with him and had seen him giving the money and the diamond. He asked why the woman lied. The man got angry. However, he could not believe that his wife was lying. He thought the villager cheated them.

He came back home and asked his wife once again. His wife swore that she was given only the money but not the diamond. They decided to file a case looking for justice to the King of the city. The King heard both sides. The villager had his witness together with him who gave his statement to the King that he had seen the villager giving the cash and the piece of diamond together. Based on the witness, the King gave his verdict in favour of the villager who cheated the couple. Because the couple lost their case, the woman was crying as they were coming from the King's palace.

After hearing the story, the herdsman King thought seriously for a while and asked all four of them turn by turn. Did you send the piece of diamond? – yes. Did you give her the diamond – yes. Did you see him giving the diamond? – yes. Did he not give you the diamond? – no, he did not give the diamond.

Then the herdsman King placed them at four different spots around the hill where they were not able to see and hear each other. He ordered, without the knowledge of the four, one of his force men to fetch fine clay. His force man brought the clay immediately. Then the herdsman king went to the four one by one, gave them a little clay and asked them to make the shape of the piece of diamond. Now the man who had given false witness statement faced a problem. He did not know what it looked like – round or flat or long. He just guessed and made a long shape. The men who sent and brought made matching shapes, but the woman did not make any shape as she had not seen it.

The herdsman king checked all one by one. When he found sender's and carrier's matching shapes but the witness man's not matching them, he knew the total truth. All four of them were brought in front of him and he ordered the man who had brought the diamond to give it to the woman. The man was carrying the piece of diamond in his pocket thinking that he had to give it if he had lost the case in front of the real King of the city. He took out the diamond from his pocket and gave it to the woman. He confessed that he had cheated because of his greed and apologised. The man who had given false witness taking money from the other man also confessed his guilt and apologised. The King punished them with ten sticks each for their crime.

'That's a fair judgement. That is justice.' I said.

'The story is not finished yet, my son.' Dad said.

People started talking about the justice provided by the herdsman King. The real King of the city also heard about it. He thought about how the herdsman could give such a justice when he could not. The real King went there with his force. When he reached the destination, the herdsmen were there as always. He saw a herdsman seated on the stone in the King's role and other herdsmen active in their respective roles. The King got the herdsman moved from the hilltop and took his seat on the stone. When he sat on the stone, he felt a different energy and a new confidence within him. He thought, 'It must be something underneath the stone for sure which gives such an energy and confidence.' He ordered his force to dig out the place. His force dug out the entire hill until it was flat, and a golden throne appeared. On the throne there were thirty-two golden

butterflies making the throne their home. When they came above ground, all thirty-two golden butterflies flew away one after another and in the end the throne also disappeared. According to the legend, after the incident the location got its name as *Battisputali* (thirty-two butterflies) because those thirty-two butterflies used to live there.

'Where did you read these stories, dad?'

'I did not read these stories from any book. My mother, your grandma, told me. She has got lots of such stories to tell. See your grandma then she will tell you many more interesting stories.'

I imagined my grandma and couldn't wait to see her. I remembered my classmates Philip, Jacob, Elina, Ade, Medha, Richard, Sylvia, Cledya, Chris, Joseph and others. I was excited at the thought of telling them these stories back in London.

CHAPTER 9

I could see a clear view of Mount Makalu from a playground above my family house in the village, my eyes could roam from east to west, and it seemed as if the whole range of white Himalayas were smiling and kissing the blue sky. This was the village where my dad was born, raised, and studied.

I had heard my dad describes the beauty of the village many times before. But I wanted to see this for myself and had waited for this moment impatiently.

It was autumn with a clear sky and clear views as far as my eyes could see. To the north, the white Himalayan range; below it, there were ranges of mountains and rolling hills with greenery; terraced landscape at the lower levels; and, at the bottoms of the mountains *Hinwa*, *Maya* and *Piluwa* rivers running like winding snakes. It was more attractive than an artist's creation. I did not want to look away for a moment.

The beautiful pictures of the village were imprinted on my eyes and heart, forever. I knew that I would have a chance to show these views to my friends in my upcoming presentation in London. And so, I took lots of photographs.

I was not satisfied only with the view from that playground. I had to look around; I had to have the views from the top of the hills, too. I knew that there might be places of historical, religious and cultural importance. I had to go and visit them all, see them all and understand them all. I knew there might be stories related to the history, cultures and traditions – I had to hear them all.

Where do I start? I thought I should plan my time in the village.

'I had a month ahead of me in the village and I knew that the initial days might be a challenged – new places, new people and new circumstances. I thought about making friends to guide me. And I was grateful that although I was born and brought up in London, my parents had taught me the Nepalese language as my first language at home. 'At least I won't have a language problem.', I thought.

CHAPTER 10

'Dad, I have to make friends, to talk to me and take me around and to guide me for sightseeing. Who can I ask?'

'Don't worry.' he said. 'I'll call Sweta from next door and she will collect some other friends. Sweta is my uncle's granddaughter, your cousin. She is only two months older than you.'

Dad went to our neighbours. He came over with Sweta in a while. Sweta had known that I was coming from London and was waiting to see me. We had never met before.

'Sweta, Robin wants to make some friends to travel around with. Now, can you collect your other friends and say hello?' Dad asked Sweta.

'Yes, of course.' Sweta replied happily.

In about half an hour she came back with five other friends. She introduced them all to me – Eashan, Rachana, Nirav, Sachin and Sirjana. It was Saturday and they were free. Sweta and all other five were in the same class, year nine. I was also in year nine in London.

After we got introduced to each other, I explained to them my interests and the desire to visit different places. I mentioned about my project that my teacher had given to me. I also mentioned that I needed to take notes of any important points and take photographs of different views that I would see. Then I wanted to have a photo of the group of my friends that would be accompanying me during my stay in the village. I asked my dad to take a picture of our group. We all took positions for the photographs in two rows. In the front row there were girls sitting on the ground. From left to right, there were Sweta, Sirjana and Rachana. We boys stood in the back row. From left to right, were Eashan, Nirav, I and Sachin. We took position in such a way that no one blocked anyone else. Dad looked through the camera and said 'smile.' We all smiled lightly, and he took a couple of snaps of the group.

CHAPTER 11

My small slim camera was an attraction to my new friends.

'How much did it cost, Robin?' Rachana asked after we reached a *Chautaro* (a traditional platform built by paving stones and planting big banyan trees for shed as a trekkers' rest point) called *Dadegaundo* (the name of the *Chautaro*) and started our talk.

'My dad bought it for me before we left London. I'm not sure how much did it cost. He told mom that he got it in a sale. He might have paid sixty to seventy pounds, I guess.'

'How much would that be in Nepalese currency?' She again expressed her curiosity.

'I haven't a clue. We will ask my dad when we go back home.' I wanted to finish this subject then and there.

All of my friends took the camera in their hands one at a time turn by turn and had a look with a lot of interest.

At the end, Sachin took it and asked having a look, 'Can I take a photograph with your camera, Robin?'

'Of course, you can Sachin. Take as many photos as you want. All of you can take some photos if you want. The camera will not break while you take the photos. Nor do we need any photo reel, it's a digital camera. We can even delete photos if they are no good.' I encouraged them and showed them how to use it.

It was normal for me to use a camera. In London, almost all my friends have seen and used a camera. It was not a big deal. But I found the situation different in the village. For them, it was a dream to use. So, all my new friends used the camera with interest turn by turn and took many snaps of those stunning natural scenes.

By the time my friends had used my camera, I had become part of the group. Now, it had become easier for me to drive them towards my goal.

'Let's discuss and decide what to do, where to go and when to go for our visits.' I proposed. All of them then looked at each other and Nirav opened the discussion, 'we have to go to school and won't be free from Sunday to Friday. We can be with you all day on Saturdays. How many Saturdays you will be here, Robin?'

'I will be here for four weeks. So, I will be here for four Saturdays including today.' I told them.

'Then let's visit the places today in and around the village. Next Saturday we will go to the *Siddhakali* temple, the following Saturday we will go to the *Baneshwor* hill and the last Saturday we will visit the *Waleshwor* cave.' Sachin made a brief plan. All my other new friends agreed with him. I was completely in the dark about everything having never been to any of the places.

'Ok then, let's start today's visit from *Gadhidanda* (one of the hilltops in the village).' Sirjana said, who had kept quiet until then. Following Sirjana's suggestion, we started climbing up to the hilltop.

CHAPTER 12

I had heard people saying Nepal is a piece of heaven on earth and they were right. From the peak of the hill, the whole panoramic view was clear and pleasing. With such stunning views, I was so amazed that I forgot myself for a moment. It was as if an artist had used his brushes and colours on his canvass or, it was a beautiful collage.

Autumn's clear weather had helped to make the views clearer and wider. White Himalayan ranges to the north and just below rows of high and low ranges of mountains; green mountains of *Ankhibhuin*, *Shanishchare* and *Madi* to the south; the view of the 'S' shaped beautiful settlement of *Chainpur* through to the high *Milke* hill to the east; from *Aurnthan* to the peak of *Baneshwor* hill to the west; blocks of green forests and villages on the slopes of the hills in all directions exactly like the beautiful prints on the dresses in a fashion show; two rivers *Piluwa* and *Hinwa* running continuously on two sides of the hill like two plaits of radiant hair of a pretty girl; it was as if a Fairy Angel had landed on earth. I tried to capture the alluring landscapes in my mind, eyes and heart. I was lost in the beauty of the nature.

'Where have you been, Robin?' Sweta touched my arm and took me out of my imaginary world.

'I was lost in these beautiful views. They are so amazing! I'd never seen such beauty before.'

'You can see even wider and clearer from the peak of the *Baneshwor* hill', Eashan spoke. But I was assured that we had already planned to visit the *Baneshwor* hill as well.

It was then that I had a brilliant new idea. 'Guys, I was originally planning to use the photographs for my project presentation. But what if I take as many photographs as I can and organise a photo exhibition in my school inviting everyone?'

'Fantastic! What a brilliant idea! It'll really be a wonderful exhibition, won't it?', said Sachin.

Other friends mirrored Sachin's enthusiasm. I felt encouraged by their positive feedback. I thought that I would have at least two to three thousand photos by the end of my trip and could select two to three hundred of the best ones. I started capturing all the panoramic views of that piece of heaven on earth with my camera: click, click, click.

CHAPTER 13

We spent about an hour on the hilltop. Sweta had brought roasted maize and soybeans from home and Sirjana had brought roasted groundnut. We sat on the ground in a circle and enjoyed eating the food together with the pleasant Autumn sunshine and talked about many things. My friends asked me to tell them about London. I described the things I like in London. The views from the Shard and London Eye, Madame Tussauds and the wax work in it, the London Underground Trains, Double Decker Buses and so on.

I described the River Thames. 'It flows from the heart of the city of London. The river is so wide and deep that large and tall ships also come into the city by this river. Passenger cruises and clippers also run where we can travel by buying tickets. Did you know? This river was a smaller river in width originally. It was made bigger by human efforts.' I did not forget to mention that the Tower Bridge is the folding one to allow tall ships to pass through. I also told them that there are ferries and tunnels instead of bridges to cross the river. I described castles and many other places that I had visited and knew about.

'Can you explain how Tower Bridge folds for tall ships, Robin?', Nirav was curious.

'Sure, I will. The construction of Tower Bridge is such that two halves from two sides are joined at the middle to make a single bridge. Both sides of the bridge can be folded and unfolded as needed. Normally, you don't feel that the bridge is made by joining two parts and people or vehicles run through as on an ordinary bridge. When there are tall ships coming which cannot pass underneath the bridge, then people and vehicles are stopped at both sides, the bridge is broken at the middle and two parts rise at two sides of the river giving room for the tall ships to pass through. After the ships have gone, both parts are brought down and joined back to the normal condition.' I gave a brief description on how the bridge operates.

'Thank you, Robin. That's interesting.' Nirav remarked.

When I told them about O2 arena at North Greenwich, they looked at me with wonder in their eyes. 'There is a cluster of houses within a big tent, where there are restaurants, cinema hall, a covered hall for games, funs for children, and much more. There is a cable car line in operation close to it'. I told them some facts I knew about the Observatory in Greenwich, too. Such as, it was established by King Charles II in AD 1675 with a purpose to study planets. Where daily time signal was initiated by dropping a time ball since 1833 AD, which was developed further as hourly time signals instead of daily after almost ninety years, i.e., since 1924 and this was called Greenwich Time Signal. BBC Radio used this signal since then as their beeping time signal and later by BBC television, too.

I shared with them happy moments I spent on the beaches by the sea, snowfall in London and playing in the snow making snowmen, London's lifestyle and so on. I told them about Notting Hill Carnival. I elaborated it, 'This festival is celebrated in London as a common festival among different communities for three days in the month of August every year. The celebration of this festival started from 1960's. Although it initially had a Caribbean flavour, there has been increased participation of locals and other communities at the later stage. Every year around one million people from across different communities attend the festival making it one of the biggest festivals of the world. People wear different costumes, masks and decorations, play drums and other musical instruments and exhibit traditional cultures. The participants gather and move into the streets.'

After listening carefully to me, Sachin commented, 'It seems that London's Notting Hill Carnival and our *Chainpur*'s *Gaijatra* (cow festival) and *Hilejatra* (mud festival) are similar in many ways.' He described, 'These festivals are celebrated for two days every year in the month of August as well, as a common festival of the local communities. Locals as well as people from other villages come to celebrate and observe the festival. *Lakhe* dance (a typical traditional dance wearing mask and special colourful costumes), performances to blow the negative aspects of the society on the day of *Hilejatra* and singing and dancing all day and night are the charms of those festivals. Although

traditionally the *Gaijatra* relates to a specific community, it has been developed as a common festival of all local communities for the past several years where they exhibit their traditional cultures together.'

While talking about different things, I took plenty of photographs whatever I found interesting and eye catching from the hilltop. Spending about an hour there, we started climbing down the hill. While climbing down we took a different route through the forest of *Khalanga*. Just before starting to climb down the hill, Sirjana explained some historical facts about the hill and the forest. She told, '*Gadhidanda* and the next hill were forts of *Gorkhali* army where they stationed to fight against the Tibetian attack long before in the history and the *Gorkhali* army defeated the Tibetians. You can still find ruins of the fort on the other hilltop, which we will see on the way down when we go to visit the *Baneshwor* hill. The *Gorkhali* army men planted and generated this forest which is now known as the forest of *Khalanga*. Actually, *Khalanga* means army in local language. Hence, the forest of *Khalanga* means the forest of army. *Gadhidanda* itself means a fort hill, where there was a fort of the *Gorkhali* army.'

We reached a place called *Jogidanda* climbing down from the hilltop. I had eye catching views from that spot as well. Mountains, slopes, greenery, farm fields, villages and so on. Sirjana started telling me the names of the villages seen from *Jogidanda*, 'That is *Ambote*, and then *Bhanjyangkhark*, on the other side *Hitidanda*, *Damaidanda*, up there *Pallogaun*, *Paudelgaun*, *Dangigaun* and *Kerabari*; on the next hill across the river are *Wana*, *Lingling Phapung*, *Archale* and so on. Whether I would remember and note down all those names or not, I couldn't say. However, when I heard names of those villages, I reflected the names of many places in London such as Charlton Village, Blackheath Village, Maze Hill, Shooters Hill, Notting Hill and found same way to give names. *Gaun* in the local language means Village whereas *Danda* means Hill.

We returned from *Jogidanda* and walked into the main settlement of *Chainpur,* went to two schools and reached the top end of the settlement. What a beautiful settlement! In between two rows of houses from top to bottom there were slate like large flat stone pieces beautifully paved making attractive front yard of the houses all the way without gap and equally beautiful steps on the slopes. Whoever visits this village will be spellbound.

In the middle of the settlement, there were houses of a specific ethnic community who make bronze products manually, which is their traditional occupation. They make daily use utensils as well as beautifully carved décor items. How beautiful were those décor products: *Karuwa* (water jug with spout), *Amkhora* (water jug without spout), *Anti* (wine jar with spout), Wine Cups and Teacup Plate sets. My friends and the producers said that those items were immensely popular. Especially, *Chainpur's Karuwa* is widely famous. I thought: 'I'll ask dad and mom to buy some of them and take them back to London. It will be really fascinating to show such artistic items from my families' village to my friends in London. If I will organise an exhibition in my school, these items will be an attraction as well.'

It was already four O'clock in the afternoon when we came back home. 'Children, you must be feeling hungry. Wash your hands and get ready for your afternoon meal.' My aunt had got it ready for us. I should mention that the daily eating pattern here in the village is quite different from that we have in London.

Normally, we have breakfast, lunch and dinner pattern in London. But, here in the village there is no breakfast like what we have in London. Instead, there is a main meal before ten o'clock in the morning (normally between nine to ten). There is no lunch in the afternoon but there is another main meal in the evening. In between two main meals of the morning and the evening, there is afternoon meal which is not like a lunch but lighter and normally is eaten between three to five in the afternoon. This was what my aunt had prepared for us.

Mouth-watering! Semolina *Haluwa* and mustard green leaf vegetable were so tasty. *Haluwa* is like couscous. It is mainly made of Semolina flour and occasionally of rice flour. While cooking *Haluwa*, the flour is first fried in butter and water is added and cooked. Sugar is another ingredient which some people prefer to add while being fried and some other people while being cooked after adding water. It can be topped up with fried cashew nuts, raisins or almonds.

Mom joined us to eat. My sister and grandma had already eaten together. While we were having our food, I could see my grandma just a bit away looking at me with her smiling face. Dad, who had gone to see his friends, came in when we had almost finished. Uncle and aunty, my dad's brother and sister-in-law, were waiting for dad and then they had their meal together. While they were having it, mom said, 'What a tasty vegetable of green leaves! I think we should have maize flour *Dhindo* with the mustard green leaf vegetable in our dinner, too.' *Dhindo* is a typical Nepalese dish made of flour, mainly of maize or millet or wheat flour. It is famous among the Nepalese families and many prefer it as a main meal. Cooking Dhindo is so easy. Required amount of water is boiled and the flour is added little by little but stirring thoroughly and continuously until it is fully cooked. When cooked, it looks, and its texture is, like a dough.

I am familiar with both dishes, *Haluwa* and *Dhindo* as my mom makes them occasionally in London. I like them as well.

'Not a problem. I will make whatever dinner you wish. Do the children and Om like it as well?' Aunty asked.

'Yes, we all like it. We do have such dinner occasionally in London, too. But we don't have such a tasty mustard leaf over there. If we have whey on top of it, it would be fantastic.' Mom replied without pausing. Thus, the menu for the dinner was fixed, too.

When dad had finished having his food, I said to him, 'Dad, when I was on the top of the *Gandhidanda* hill earlier, an idea formed in my mind after viewing the amazing scenes. My friends liked and supported it. What you think, please advise me'.

'Tell me. I will definitely advise you.'

'I've taken lots of photographs of such beautiful scenes and will keep on taking pictures wherever I go. I will include some of them in my project presentation. Apart from the classroom presentation, I'll ask my teacher to organise a photo exhibition in the school. I hope that my teacher will go for it. Our school always encourages pupils for such creative ideas. I saw *Chainpur's Karuwa, Amkhora* and other decor products. I am thinking of taking some of them and displaying them in the exhibition as well.'

'It's a brilliant idea. Go for it, my boy.' He encouraged me and said further, 'After hearing your idea, I want to suggest one more thing. Ask your teacher if they can organise an exhibition as a fund-raising event to support local schools here in the village. Plan to support what the schools need. I will take you to the schools tomorrow. See for yourself and discuss with the teachers to identify the areas of support. What do you think?'

'Fantastic! Such a good idea! Ok dad, I will do that.' I was so excited.

I could not wait till tomorrow, I would go to schools, and talk to the teachers. I was extremely interested to observe the schools where my dad had studied. I had visited the schools today with my friends but had only seen the buildings from the outside. I was keen to see classrooms and see how the classes were run, too. I was happy that this wish of mine was going to be fulfilled as a reason had emerged, too.

After our chat about this issue, I and my friends went to my grandma and sat in front of her to hear stories from her. I had been dreaming of doing this since I had left London.

CHAPTER 14

My grandma! She had already crossed eighty-five years of age. The overlapping wrinkles on her face are, perhaps, piled up experiences of her life. Or, they are mathematics of her happiness and sorrows. Or, perhaps they were pages of her stories of success and failure, pride and regret, self-esteem and compromises of love and hates. Although there were wrinkles all over her face, she was always smiling. Her lips, which were pushed inside into her toothless mouth, were always on the verge of a smile, like the pleasant light of the full moon.

I used to wish long life for grandma whenever my parents talked about her. When Philip had told me about his holiday last year and that he visited his grandparents in Peterborough and the stories they told him, I had felt impatient to see my grandma. Perhaps, I was jealous of him and just did know it. My grandpa was not alive. He died long before I was born. At home, my parents talked only about my grandma who was thousands of miles away remembering us and climbing final steps of her life ladder. I feared she might also die before I saw her.

Leaving all those fears in London, I was now in the village, in front of my grandma. I had already had her loving hugs and pampering. I had already been wrapped in unlimited happiness. When we reached home, she hugged me and my sister tightly, and said, 'pieces of my heart' and kissed all over our faces. She said with joy, 'Your father never brought you; he always said he would bring; now you are here, and I can see you.' She was so happy. 'I always feared if I could not have chance to see you. Perhaps, this is what loving the interest more than the principal means.' Saying this, she laughed her toothless mouth opening wide with joy and happiness, which I will always remember.

CHAPTER 15

My grandma was just seven years old when she got married. There was a tradition of child marriage in those days. There was a social value that daughters should get married before they experience menarche. Many used to get married even at the age of five. How could the feet which had just left mothers' laps be happy in unknown people's house? Or, were they allowed to play with childhood freedom in those unknown house yards? I felt sad thinking of that. 'This is unfair to the children and injustice against them', I kept my thoughts to myself.

'How did you accept that you would get married at that age?', I asked grandma.

'How would I know? They dressed me up like a beautiful doll. I was so happy to have those new and nice dresses and jewellery. I was thinking that my friends, who were standing close to me, were looking at me jealously. Time to time during that function, I used to run with my friends and my father and brother used to catch me and bring back to the stage. A priest was reciting verses on the other side of the stage which I did not understand at all. Our neighbours and many other villagers were around to watch that drama. There were also many people whom I did not know. I knew later when I reached the age to be able to understand all those things that they were bridegroom's family and friends. I was happy then that I was a beautiful doll in a doll's game. When I reached the age that I was able to understand, I knew that it was not a doll's game. Rather, it was my marriage ceremony. After the function, I was carried in a traditional bridal carriage, *Doli* in the local language, to my new home, the groom's house, walking two days. My father and brother also accompanied the bridegroom but did not stay over here and returned the same day of our arrival. People had a belief that fathers were not allowed culturally even to drink water of their daughter's married home.' Grandma told her marriage story.

My grandma's parent's house was on the other side of the next mountain across the river. It would take two days to reach there walking down to the bottom of the hill, then up to the top of the other mountain and again down. When she was a little girl, it would not be possible for her to go there alone even if she wanted to.

When she grew up and was able to travel alone, she told that she frequently visited her parents. However, she has spent almost eight decades of her life in this house. She had only a blur memory of the moments she spent in her parent's house while she was young.

I asked her again, 'Was grandpa also the same age as your, when you got married to him?'

'Nope, he was a big man, twenty-three-year-old. Rather, his son or my stepson was almost of my age, six years old, just one year younger than me. He was born when your grandpa was seventeen. He used to beat me; he had a violent nature. He wanted everything his own way. When grown up, he respected and loved me a lot. He even admitted how much pain and trouble he knew he had caused me. When he had his own family, he migrated to the southern plain part of Nepal called *Madhesh*. But he came to see us almost every year. He died of cancer just within two months of your grandpa's death. One year before he died, he had come to see us and he had brought lots of clothes and sweets for me', when she remembered her stepson, her eyes were filled with tears and she wiped them away with the corner of her shawl.

My grandma was herself a collection of stories of her happiness and sadness. I asked her to share with me memorable incidents of her life. She started telling one after another.

'Fine, I'll tell you the incident related to my birth, which I was told by my mother when I was well grown up and had gone to see her. She said that I was born at a moment of an odd planetary situation. Anyone born during such planetary alignment is regarded as bad luck for the family. So, my father told someone to throw me off from a cliff close to our house. My father's uncle from next door was also present at the time, who was also a good astrologer, reacted and questioned him what he was saying. He had already calculated my birth chart and had found that I was the most fortunate all the other children for the family. He told my father that not all are bad luck if born in such a planetary situation. Instead, some are wealth giving. Your daughter is one of such children and your new-born daughter is, in fact, a fortune for wealth. See, how much you will earn from now on because of her fortune. If still you think her a misfortune, give her to me, I'll bring up as my daughter. Then, my father looked at me saying she is my goddess of wealth. True to his prediction, my father started earning a lot and bought lands here in the hill as well as in the *Madhesh* (the plain region of our country) and became a rich man. Your grandpa was also not a rich man before marrying me. After I came to this house, he earned quite a lot and became a rich man, too, which I heard from my mother-in-law.' While explaining her birth incident I could clearly see a smile of pride on her lips.

Sharing another incident of her life related to her marriage she told, 'Listen, I must tell you another incident related to my marriage, which my mother-in-law told me when I was grown up. I am the second wife of your grandfather. His first wife died when she was pregnant for the second time. She suddenly suffered from massive bleeding. In those days, there was a practice of treating any patient with local herbs and the shamans or the faith healers. A shaman chanted day and night playing his typical drum, but the poor girl was just twenty years old when she left this world in front of eyes of everyone who were present there. Two years had passed after her death when your grandfather married me. When they came to see me with the marriage proposal, our birth calendars did not match to each other. But your grandfather was an interesting man. He did not believe in the birth calendars; he tore them up and threw them in the river and then he married me.

CHAPTER 16

When we were listening to my grandma's stories, I was upset by the issues of child marriage and lack of medical facilities to deal with the pregnancy care. She had paused and we were waiting for her to speak. When she was ready, she said, 'I want the answer from Robin, and I am asking him. The rest of you do not say anything.'

'A small tree that hurts if you try to climb it. What is that?' She asked and smiled.

Suddenly getting such a puzzling question, I was confused as to what to say. I did not know the answer. I knew it was a fun riddle, but I had never had any chance to play Nepalese riddles in London. So, I replied, 'I do not know its answer. Please tell me.'

'So, you don't know? Then offer me a village and I'll tell you the answer.' She said. I got more confused and puzzled.

'What are you saying? I do not understand. What do you mean by offering a village?' I asked again. I did not know any practice of offering a village while playing riddles. This was something completely new to me.

'Then, you don't know the answer. You must offer me a village to get the answer of the riddle I've asked. Didn't you know about offering a village?'

'No, I have never heard about this type of puzzle. Please explain, what is this all about.' I expressed my lack of understanding.

Then she explained, 'While playing riddles, if the listeners cannot answer the question asked, they should offer a village to the teller. Then the teller keeps all good things of the village offered with them and they leave all bad or rubbish things for the listeners. Finally, the teller gives the answer of the puzzle. So, if you don't know the answer of the puzzle, I've asked you, offer me a village and I'll give you the answer.

Now, I came to know about the meaning of offering a village. I learnt a typical new method of playing riddles. Why did my parents not teach me such an interesting thing? I got angry with them. However, I learnt from my grandmother. Thanks to her. 'I offer you our village. Please tell me, what does that mean?' After offering village, I looked at her for the answer.

With a victorious smile on her face, grandma started explaining the puzzle, 'Every good thing of this village is mine, no, no, they all are yours (perhaps she wanted to give every good thing to her lovely grandson!). All the rubbish things to a demon. The answer of this puzzle is a nettle plant, a stinging nettle. The nettle plant is small but if you touch it, it stings. So, the puzzle says that a small tree hurts if you try to climb it.'

Fantastic! An interesting way of raising knowledge.

'Now, another riddle. Only one leaf of a straight tree, what is it?'

Grandma had already told my friends not to speak. They were looking at me. I was the only one who had to answer the puzzle.

I did not know the answer of that puzzle, too and offered grandma the neighbouring village. She blessed me with all the good things of the village, the rubbish things she gave to the demon again and answered the puzzle that it's a big spoon with long handle which is used for stirring rice while cooking.

'One more but the last one. It's a truth, it exists but neither we need it, nor we can see it when we want. What is that?' Grandma asked me another puzzle.

I did not have answer for that puzzle either. Hence, I offered her London in place of a village.

'Every good thing of London is yours. All rubbish things to the demon. The answer of this puzzle is an earthquake.' Once again, she smiled, and her face shined with happiness.

'You know when an earthquake occurs nobody knows. Everybody knows it may happen. But nobody knows where it exists, and we do not need it at all. Rather it is destructive, and nobody wants it to happen. Now I'll tell you about an earthquake episode that happened in our village when I was still a young girl and how I survived.'

'Please tell us.' We replied as we were eager to listen.

Superb! What an interesting method my grandma used to raise the subject; she was like an experienced teacher. I remembered my teachers. They also use different methods to create interests of the students before they raise the topics. My grandmother used a similar method. My teachers are educated people trained on teaching methods. My grandma! She was an illiterate old village lady. Where did she get such brilliant skill? Perhaps, it was her intuitive talent. Or, did it derive from her life experiences, which I could see marked as numerous wrinkles on her face.

She started describing the incident, 'I was just twelve years old. But I was the only daughter-in-law of the family. I had to go to fetch grass for the cattle and kitchen fuel from the forest. My mother-in-law used to warn your grandfather not to send me alone for all those type of work as I

was still a young girl. She used to love me a lot. But your grandpa never cared what she said. On that day, too, I had gone to the forest called *Fukuwa* down at the bottom of the hill alone to fetch kitchen fuel.'

'I finished collecting fuel and was climbing up the hill with a load on my back to return home. Opposite of the forest site, I had just reached up to a rest point called *Khirrachautaro*, the earth suddenly started shaking. Initially, I thought that the load I was carrying was unbalanced. But this was a different matter. The earth shook more and more violently. My body was unbalanced, and the load of fuel dropped from my back. It rolled down to the bottom of the hill and scattered. I fell down, and I tried to stand up again and again but fell down every time. I fell down into the rocky ravine which I had crossed just before the earth started shaking. I was badly hurt and bleeding. I felt the warmth of my blood. I held strongly to a small tree to save myself.' She seemed that her pain was refreshed while she was telling the story.

The story was not ended, yet. She described a further scary situation, 'Not only did the earth shake but at the same time I heard a loud odd sound of a landslide. In front of my eyes, the forest where I had collected fuel a while ago started sliding down along with the village on the top of it. I saw houses, farmland and the forest sliding down. I also heard birds, cattle and the people screaming and crying loudly. In that situation I was alone, a poor little girl. I thought that I would not survive. I was shaking with a wounded body and fear. I would not let go off the tree I was holding as it was the only hope of my survival. I spent every moment in fear and pain. Thank god, after some time, the shaking earth started slowing down and stopped. Then with much difficulty, I started climbing up the hill to go home. I reached another rest point called *Simalichautaro* and laid down on a flat stone to take a rest.'

After a while, your grandfather came along with other four people looking for me. I noticed that your grandpa was happy to see me alive. I was seriously injured and could not walk myself and your grandpa carried me on his back all the way up to our house. Seeing me in that condition, my mother-in-law came close to me pushing back other people and started comforting me with her loving and caring hand on my head and shoulder. She scolded your grandpa and asked why he did not listen to her not to send me alone in the forest. She started taking care of me and I got treatment with the local medicinal herbs. It took almost a month for me to completely recover. Many people had died, and many houses were ruined that day. Thank god, our house was safe except some minor cracks.

Later in London, I researched about that earthquake online and found out that that was one of the biggest earthquakes in Nepal. The day that earthquake devastated Nepal was on 1934 January 15. At 2:28 pm local time, an 8 magnitude on the Richter scale the earthquake had occurred and the epicentre was *Chainpur*, my parental village. The earthquake took the lives of more than seventeen thousand people. Thousands of houses were destroyed, and hundreds of thousand people became homeless.

From the study, I also learnt that another big earthquake in 1255 AD had hit Nepal. This took lives of more than thirty thousand people of Kathmandu including the then King of the city Abhaya Malla and this number was one third of the population then in Kathmandu. I also learnt that Nepal is situated in the most earthquake prone region on the earth.

CHAPTER 17

I found my grandmother had a strong character even though she had quite a lot of different experiences of pain and sorrow in her life. I found it interesting to listen to each one of her stories. One afternoon, I was talking to her. An old lady from the neighbouring village came over to see her and they started chatting. The old lady said, 'My granddaughter was born two days ago. She is so cute and lovely. But, you know, her mother suffered so much to give birth. She had labour pains for five days and on one occasion she nearly died. However, the traditional birth attendant was so experienced that she handled everything for a safe delivery. She told that she had taken training on safe delivery methods, too. She never left my daughter-in-law unattended until she gave birth and saved her. Even now she is taking care of her and she visits her two times a day.'

'What is wrong with today's women?', grandma reacted. 'But, it may all depend on individual woman's body condition. For me, the case is different. I gave birth one after another without any complications. In some cases, I even gave birth on the farmland, too. For example, when Robin's father was born, I even did not feel much labour pain. There were labour women working that day in the field picking millet. I was serving afternoon meal to them. I felt a slight pain in the lower part of my tummy. I knew that my labour had started. I mentioned it to them and told them I needed to go home. I asked one of them to collect and bring all the pots and utensils used for the snacks once they finish. I asked two women to go with me to help me if anything happens on the way back home. But our house was just a few minutes away on foot. Soon we reached home. Those two women prepared a place for delivery at a corner of kitchen lounge. I felt a strong pain but for just a while and Robin's father was born.' After saying this, grandma laughed aloud.

'How many children did you have grandma?'

'One dozen. Seven are still alive.'

'If only seven are alive, then what happened to the other five?' I again asked her.

Perhaps, my question scratched an old wound of her pain in her heart. Her smiling face suddenly turned dark. She took a long breath and told, 'Two were miscarried when I was three and four months pregnant. I do not have much recollection about them. But a son and a daughter died at the ages of ten and eight years. They both were so cute, cheerful and active. That time, we were in *Dandagaun*, one of our farm field villages. An episode of measles broke out in the village and there was no medical facility. The death demon filched those two blooming buds of my heart one after another just two days apart. I felt that my heart was crushed and cried for many days with unbearable pain. I even lost my mind for many days; I was like a mad person. I did not want to stay any longer in that village and immediately returned home taking all other children with me. I had eight children left until a few years back when my second eldest daughter died. She died in her sixties but was too young to die, yet. The death demon should have taken me in her place.

Perhaps, my grandma's heart had been broken again remembering her beloved children, I had brought back all her love she had for them. She could not stop herself and tear drops fell from her eyes and splashed her cheeks.

My grandma! She had had unmeasurable sorrow and pain. She is the root of my existence. I felt a deep love for her which I had never felt before. I wiped off her tears with my both hands. I held both her cheeks with my palms, told her not to cry and gave a kiss on her forehead. My expression of love in this way reassured her. She wiped off her tears with a corner of her shawl and, smiled while looking at me. I also smiled to give her comfort.

CHAPTER 18

My dad had said that grandma had some favourite stories which she loved to tell again and again. Her story telling style was interesting which I already had witnessed a while ago when she started with some riddles to tell the story of the earthquake. Another interesting thing about her is that she used to link all her stories to herself whether the incidents had happened to herself or she had heard the stories from others. How good is that!

We were waiting for another story when she suddenly asked, 'Are you scared of ghosts?'

'Yes grandma, we are scared', Rachana replied.

'Oh, because I was thinking of telling a ghost story. Maybe, I should not be telling it, then?'

'No, no. We are scared when we see a ghost. I did not mean that we are scared to listen to a story. We are not scared at all to listen. What do you say friends?', Rachana immediately replied.

'Yah, yah. We are not scared of the ghost story. Tell us grandma', The rest of us told grandma in one voice.

'Ok then. I'll tell it. Listen carefully', Grandma was ready to tell the story. We had nearly missed it, but it was fine now.

We nodded our heads and listened to her.

'We're a farming family. Our routine work included farming, rearing cattle, collecting grass for the cattle and collecting fuel for our kitchen, milling with traditional equipment and so on', she started. 'We had two milking cows and two milking buffaloes. In addition to grass and hay, we used to feed them with maize flour soup once a day for more milk. In those days, we did not have mechanical mills like today. We had to rely on traditional hand grinder made up of two heavy round pieces of stone called *Janto* in local language to grind maize for the flour. Unfortunately, we did not have the maize grinder in our own house, and we had to go to our neighbours. I used to do that job myself as there was no one else in the family to do it. My children had not yet grown up. It was unusual to send my mother-in-law and there was no practice in the village of doing that job by men'. She clarified the background of the story and paused for a while. We were listening to her spellbound.

'On one occasion, the maize flour was completely used up to feed the cattle. I had to go to a house called *Dandaghar* (hilltop house in local language) belonging to one of our relatives to make maize flour'. We became more curious as grandma continued with story. She mentioned, 'That day we had work from the early morning for ploughing and preparing the land. I would not be able to prepare a meal on time for the labourers and the family members if I had not started cooking early that morning. So, I decided to have maize flour ready and come back home before it was dawn'.

'What time do you mean by before dawn grandma?', I asked her to get a clear idea of time.

'I don't know, what time exactly it was. In those days, we did not have watches like today. We used to rely on the cocks' early crows to know about daybreak. I woke up at the first cock crow; freshened up myself; filled up a bamboo basket with maize and then set out'. Grandma clarified about time in her own way.

'It was a full moon. There was enough moonlight outside to see the path. I had a bamboo basket filled with maize and carried it on my waist; came out of house; opened our compound gate which was made with bamboo culms and branches and closed it back. You know that the trail from our house to the playground on the hilltop runs along a gully. As soon as I started walking up along the gully, I saw abnormally big man completely nude, sitting on the ground with his legs folded and playing two strange but small puppet like images on his hands. The two images were shining with two different colours. One on his right hand was shining with blue colour and the other one on his left hand with red colour. He had his two wooden pots, specially made for making and keeping yoghurt at homes, which he had placed to his right and left each. I had heard about people who were known for summoning ghosts or evil spirits. I had also heard that these people summon the ghosts or the evil spirits and instruct them to harm someone whom they want to. The spirits obey their instructions.' While grandma was describing the scenario, my friends were unknowingly moving slowly closer to each other.

'Looking at the scene, I thought that the man was someone from the village who was summoning the evil spirits, probably to harm my family, and they were the colourful images in his hands. I decided to chase him away.'

Grandma kept on telling further the story, 'I started shouting at him – shameless guy, why you don't feel shame to be nude like this sitting in others' street, go away right now. After I shouted at him, the shining images disappeared from his hands and then he poured the yoghurt from his both pots on the ground which flowed down towards me and he stood up carrying those pots by one hand. I saw him abnormally tall. I had never noticed such a tall man in our village and thought that he might be from a different village. When he stood up, he reached up to the playground in one step, caught a branch of a big banyan tree which was in one corner of it, then leapt to the other side of the hill with his second step and disappeared'.

I noticed my friends huddled to each other. Perhaps, they were scared. But I was enjoying the story. Grandma was telling without stopping, 'When he disappeared, I slowly walked up towards the playground. I became cautious about the yoghurt he had poured and was prepared to jump over it if needed. But strange! As I walked up close to the spot, I did not see any sign of yoghurt on the ground anymore. I took no notice and thought it might have dried up and been absorbed by the soil. I was carrying a load on my waist, so I could not walk fast and walked up slowly. When I reached the playground, it was flat, not sloped anymore, and easier to walk to reach the hilltop house. There was the district court office building close to the banyan tree and there were two nightguards on duty. Those nightguards also saw that tall man leapt catching a branch of the banyan tree. Then immediately they saw me going towards the hilltop house. As I was preparing the grinder to grind maize, they arrived. Actually, they had come to check if I was scared.'

Grandma's story telling style was unique. She used to tell every detail without missing out any. Because of this, I felt I was moving along with the story and that helped me to store everything in my mind clearly.

'So, you're here for grinding maize, madam? Saying this, they took their seats in front of me. I simply replied – yes. Then they asked – did you see that tall man leap over the other side of the hill catching the banyan tree? I replied – yes, I saw that shameless man. He was completely nude. I explained everything to them what I saw and said – I don't think that he was from our village. After listening to me, one of them said – ma'am, it was not a normal human being. It could be a ghost or a spirit or a god. When he told that then I was scared, and I turned cold. I started shivering. I could not continue grinding maize.' In this way, she told the story bringing the incidents one after another.

'But, don't be scared and calm down ma'am. It seems it was not an evil spirit or any ghost. That's why he easily gave in and didn't scare you. He might be an angel and he might have wanted to fetch a good fortune to your family in the form of yoghurt to bless your family with wealth. They were reassuring me, but I was shivering with fear.' While grandma was explaining her condition, she was also expressing her fear gesturing with her hands, face and body language. She was speaking continuously, 'Then they asked me to stop grinding maize and they offered help that they would ask their women to do that for me. They asked me to go home and accompanied me instead of letting me go home alone. When we reached home, my husband and mother-in-law asked what had happened. I described everything I had seen, and the nightguards also explained the incident. After listening to us, my mother-in-law reassured me – don't be scared, what you saw is not an evil spirit but that was an angel. Now our family will have blessings of fortune. My mother-in-law told me that she had also once seen similar tall man near our house. After that, my father-in-law made a good progress wealth wise. Now our family will have good things to see again. Don't get scared. Hearing my mother-in-law's remarks, I felt reassured and I was afraid no more.' In the end she said, 'the person that I had thought was summoning ghosts was himself a ghost' and laughed aloud opening full her toothless mouth.

'You did not fall ill, grandma? People say that encountering a spirit people fall ill', Nirav asked grandma.

'No, not at all. Nothing happened to me. After hearing my mother-in-law, my fear was completely gone. Since then, no one has seen that man. As said by my mother-in-law, perhaps that was an angel bringing good fortune for us. Happiness increased in our family and our progress gone up wealth wise. My children made good progress in their education', grandma finished telling story and wrapped it up with a rhythmic verse at the end.'

To the listeners – gold's garland
To the teller – flower's garland
May this story go direct to the god's land.

Now it was my turn to ask a question, 'Grandma, what do you mean by gold's garland, flower's garland and god's land?'

'Oh, don't you know my dear? It is a common practice to tell this verse at the end of a folklore. It is believed that both the storyteller and the listeners will benefit from good fortune by telling this verse at the end of the story', grandma explained to me.

Awesome, a new thing to learn. What an interesting way of wrapping up a story. I was so happy to learn such new techniques in addition to the story itself.

CHAPTER 19

Now, grandma was ready to tell another story.

'I'd mentioned in my story I just told you that we used to keep cattle, do you remember?', Grandma started background for another story after the one about the ghost. I liked her style of telling stories with a clear background at the beginning very much. It had helped me quite a lot to understand the stories by placing myself in the world of the story itself.

'Yes, we remember.'

'We never had less than two or three cows and/or buffaloes kept. That time, too, we had two milking cows and a buffalo. The buffalo was not milking. Out of two milking cows, one had had a calf of just two weeks. The other one was about to stop milking soon and the calf was also grown up big.'

'We don't have, and did not have that time, too, any big forest around the village where tigers or bears live. We had a small forest called *Khalanga's* forest, where there are no tigers and bears to be found. But there were plenty of jackals in this forest. Soon after dusk, they start howling. You might have also heard the jackal pack howling. One howls at the start and then the second one, then the other one and at the end many jackals including their cubs all howl together. This is called jackal pack howling. Do you know what they say in jackal pack howling? The first one says – I'm the king of this area; second suspects and says – is this true?; the third one supports the first one and says – he is right; and at the end all of them support each other including the cubs and say – that's right, absolutely right. Now, are you all clear my dears?' having said this, grandma paused herself for a while and looked smiling at us one by one. Perhaps, she was observing our interests.

'What an interesting explanation of jackal pack howling!', I praised the explanation.

'Let's come to the point. Let me talk about the tiger again. Although there is not any forest close to the village where tigers live, occasionally we hear stories of tigers from somewhere else that come into the village and attack cattle and even people. A tiger had entered the village that night when the incident happened. There was an incident the previous month when a tiger had entered the next village down the hill and killed a farmer's ploughing ox.', grandma started coming to the point of the story.

'As I said, I was the only daughter-in-law in the family and had to do all the household chores as was daughter-in-law's job traditionally. All day, I used to be busy doing this and that and never got a break until I went to bed. Starting early in the morning from cleaning the house, fetching water from the water source down the hill, collecting and fetching grass for the cattle and fuel for kitchen, preparing and serving meals to the family members and farm labourers up to four times a day and so on. I can't even list all my jobs. Until I finished cleaning up the kitchen and the utensils after the dinner, almost all of the family members would have gone to bed. But it wouldn't be yet my time to go to bed. Only after I had massaged my elderly mother-in-law's feet with mustard oil, I could go to the bed.' Grandma recalled her hard days as a daughter-in-law and explained to us in a simple way. But I did not see any regret in her with all those hard days she had. Instead, I could read a feeling of pride on her face how she had handled her home successfully.

I was listening to her with great interest. I'd already understood how meaningful and important was every word that she used. Hence, I had all my attention to her so that I could catch every single word she spoke.

'That day as well, it had already been late evening when I went to bed after I massaged my mother-in-law's feet with oil. I already told you before, we did not have watches those days and did not know what time it was. I think it was almost midnight. I fell asleep immediately after I went to the bed.' She moved further towards her story.

'You know, I've always been a light sleeper, like a dog. While sleeping, I am sensitive to even a soft sound. But, your grandpa? He had a very deep sleep'.

'I woke up with a sound of a cow mooing loudly. I thought, the cow might have been trapped in the rope she was fastened with. I got up instantly, lit a lantern and went out of the house carrying the lantern. There was a shed where the cows were kept downwards from the front yard of our house. The shed was covered with bamboo culms and branches on three sides, but the front side was open. I looked into the shed from the edge of the front yard. The cow with new-born calf was jumping aggressively, mooing loudly, and trying to break the rope she was fastened with. Another cow and the buffalo were also trying to break their ropes they were fastened with. It was a scary scene. Towards the

front of the shed, about ten yards away, I saw a tiger grabbing the new-born calf with its  paws. It was but natural that the cow, a mother of her new-born cute baby, was trying to fight with the tiger. If she could have broken the rope, she would have killed the tiger with her horns. It's a mother's love.'

'Having seen such a terrible scene, at first I got scared but did not run away. I made my heart strong, raised the lantern higher and started shouting at the tiger – leave the calf, go away. Then I called the people sleeping in the neighbourhood for help raising my sound high, help… help… a tiger has grabbed our calf, help… help… When I started shouting, the tiger glared at me. Unbelievable, what flashing eyes he had! Like light bulbs. Hearing me, my family members and neighbours immediately came over, about ten or twelve people. Some of them were carrying sticks, some lanterns and others were carrying knives, too. Seeing so many people around, the tiger left the calf and ran away. After the tiger ran away, we went to the calf and saw that the tiger had already plunged his claws into the calf's neck. There were holes all over the neck made by tiger's claws and it was bleeding from the holes. Thank god, the tiger had not got chance to suck the calf's blood. Then we carried the calf to her mother. The cow showed her love on her baby by licking her wounded neck. We left the cow to lick her baby for a while, then comforted her and brought the calf inside our house. I washed the wounds and applied some ointment made from local medicinal plants.'

'Did she survive?' I asked.

'Yes, she did. I saved her scaring away the tiger.' Grandma said and when she was saying this with pride, I could see on her face a sign of victory.

'Children, what lesson you get from this story? Whatever the trouble is, if you are strong mentally, you may find a way out from the trouble. Does not this story teach you such a lesson? If I had ran away with fear and had gone into the house, the tiger would have killed the calf immediately.' Grandma finished telling her story and paused saying 'to the listeners – gold's garland, to the teller – flower's garland' she paused leaving for us to tell the remaining phrase of the wrap up verses and we together said – 'may this story go direct to the god's land.'

Grandma had finished telling stories for the day. The sun had already set, and it had already become dusk. My friends said, 'We'll see you tomorrow at our school' and set out to go home.

After I had my dinner, I took out my notebook and checked if I had anything missed out. Then I went to bed. But my mind was full of everything. All I had seen and been told were replayed in my mind. I thought so deeply about my proposed exhibition and before I knew it, I was asleep.

CHAPTER 20

My dad and I set off early to go to the local schools.

First, we went to the upper school. Out of two schools in the village, this was located on the hilltop. The other one is located at the lower level of the hill. I'd been looking forward to visit both of these schools and meet the teachers and the students. I was thankful that my dad had been so positive, creative and encouraging.

We entered the compound of the upper school, which was a playground. Students were scattered all over the yard. Some were talking in small groups and some were playing. I did not miss the chance taking some photographs of the school building and students in the playground. Nice views were seen from the school compound, too, and I took some pictures. Seeing us as strangers, the students were looking at us. There were also the friends I had made yesterday, and they came running to see us. After we had a brief chat with them, dad and I went upstairs through the steps outside the building to the balcony to go to the head teacher's office.

It was now assembly and the prayers time. A school staff member sounded the school bell, tin... tin... tin... tin... Immediately, all the students lined up in their year groups in the yard. Boys were in white shirts, green trousers and green neck ties and the girls were in white shirts, green skirts and green neck ties. It was an awesome view of the lined-up boys and girls in their dresses from the balcony as if lotus flowers were blooming in lines on a big pond. First of all, the Physical Exercise teacher got the students to do some exercises. When the students were lined up in their uniform dresses and were doing exercises, it looked like the lotus flowers were waving in a pleasant breeze. I did not miss out the opportunity to capture those great scenes and snapped as much as I could.

When the physical exercise was over, the teacher instructed them to be ready for prayers. Then the students joined their palms, a typical Nepalese style of greeting and respect, tilted their heads downwards and got ready for prayers. The teacher said one, two, three... start and all the students sang in one voice the Nepalese National Anthem first and then *Saraswati Vandana* (a verse dedicated to the goddess of wisdom). *'Saraswati Mayadrishta Vinapustakadharini, Hansavahanasamyukta Vidyadanam Karo Tu Me* (Hey Goddess *Saraswati*, who you are holding *Vina* (a guitar like instrument) and books and sitting on the swan, please bless us with wisdom).' When hundreds of students were singing the verse together, the atmosphere became pleasantly rhythmic, too. With the rhythmic buzz they were producing, I felt like all the surrounding area was mesmerised and the trees around were dancing.

When prayers were over, the students got instruction from the teacher and went to their respective classrooms showing a high level of discipline and lined up by year groups. Then we also went into the head teacher's office.

The head teacher and all other teachers were in the office. I learnt that that was the only room available in the school to share among all the teachers including the head teacher. Dad first introduced himself and then me to all the teachers. I greeted them all with great respect by joining my both palms. After the introduction session, some of the teachers left the room carrying chalk and dusters to their classes. As my dad asked, I told the teachers about the project I was given by my teacher in London. Then I explained in detail how I would plan the idea of photo exhibition to be used as a fundraising event to support the local schools.

'There is nothing that we don't like about this plan as it benefits our school.' The Head teacher commented and said, 'What help will you need from us?' Other teachers supported the head teacher.

'I would appreciate a couple of things please. The first one we can do today.' I expressed my requests. 'The first thing I want is to visit and observe running classrooms. I want to take some photographs to include in my exhibition and I think, we can do it today. The second thing I need is to have a brief profile of the school. When was it established? How many students are here in the school? What is the ratio of boys to girls? Which grades are running? What is the percentage of absentees and dropouts and the reasons for this? What are the problems of the school? And so on. I don't need a long and detailed description. Instead, a page or a half page. A fact sheet in a single page. Would you be able to prepare this and hand it back to me in a week or two please?'

'No problem, Robin. We already have all the information and profile ready as we prepared one just last week. The only job is to copy the fact sheet. We can get it ready and hand it to you by tomorrow. Now, which year group's classroom do you want to go today for observation? Let's go now.' The head teacher was ready to go for the classroom observations after he promised for the profile.

'I'm in year nine in London. So, I would like to start my visit from year group nine's classroom. Then we will go to other classrooms. Is that okay for you sir?' I expressed my interest.

The Head Teacher took me and my dad to the classroom of year group nine. At first, I had a quick look into the classroom from the door. The classroom had a muddy floor full of dust; there were five students seated in each pair of desks and benches; on the wall opposite from the door, there was a blackboard almost totally discoloured; and, the teacher was wiping off what was written on the blackboard. I took a few photographs of all these scenarios from the door before entering the classroom. We entered the classroom along with the head teacher. All the students stood up from their seat in respect and said together 'good morning sir'. After the Head Teacher said, 'sit down', all the pupils took their seats.

I clearly observed the dust coming up from the floor while we were walking in the classroom. Although water was sprinkled earlier to suppress the dust, it was already drying up and the dust had started rising. The Head Teacher explained me that small groups of students were formed, and each group was assigned for a day to sprinkle water on the dusty floor two times every day, first in the morning when they arrive to their classrooms and the second time in the afternoon after their lunch break. The assigned group of students had to bring water in jugs from the school's water tap and they sprinkled the floor with their hands. This was the same practice as in my dad's school days, too.

The Head Teacher asked my dad and me to introduce ourselves. After dad, it was my turn and I introduced myself telling my name, my school's name and my year group to be nine. The friends I had made yesterday were present there. So, I felt comfortable to be there. I answered questions some other students asked about

London. I took more pictures, and we came out of the classroom. Then we visited two more classrooms, year eight and ten. I found the same dust problem in those classrooms as well. After visiting the classrooms, we returned to the office room.

After we took our seat in the office room, the head teacher opened the discussion, 'How did you find your visits to the classrooms, Robin?'

'It was nice to observe, sir. I found two things that need to be improved. Firstly, the floor of the classrooms. Dust was coming up from the floor while walking on the muddy floors. Students and teachers have to spend whole day in those dusty rooms which is affecting their health. Secondly, the blackboards. Almost all of them were fully discoloured and the writings are not clearly readable to the students even if the front benchers can see it. The worst thing about the blackboard is again the dust from the chalk that the teacher and student get from the use of chalk every day. I'm worried about the health of the teachers and students.' I expressed my concerns.

'Exactly Robin, you read my mind. These are the issues that we have in our mind, too. To be honest, we are the sufferers. We are currently unable to do anything due to lack of money. If we get support to improve these conditions, we will have our life changed. Mr. Om, how brilliant is your son. He could find the core problem in one look.' The head teacher was happy and expressed his appreciation.

I could read on my dad's face that he was feeling proud of me for headteacher's appreciation and remarks about me and my thoughts. Following headteacher's support, I decided to plan my project on those problems. But a single project might not be enough to address all those problems. However, I expressed what had come to mind, 'Let's make a plan to get rid of the dust in the classrooms. For that, the classrooms should have concrete floors and the blackboards should be replaced by whiteboards. How much would that cost?'

'There are ten classrooms on the ground floor. It may cost ten thousand Rupees (Nepalese currency) to have concrete floor in each classroom, thus, making a total sum of one hundred thousand Rupees. Similarly, we have a total of twenty blackboards from all the classrooms. A whiteboard will cost around three thousand Rupees including transportation, hence, making a total of sixty thousand Rupees for all twenty. This way, we will need a total budget of one hundred and sixty thousand Rupees.' The headteacher presented us with estimated budget.

I looked at and asked my dad, 'How much is it in pounds, dad?'

'Approximately, one thousand two hundred pounds.'

I took all the necessary notes of the discussion. Then we said goodbye to the teachers and set off for the lower school. It was the lunch break when we reached the lower school. The students were scattered and playing in the school compound. I took some photographs of the scenes of the school and students from a distance. Like in the upper school, we visited the classrooms and discussed the problems. I found that the lower school had same problems as of the upper school and they needed the same amount of money as well. We spent around an hour and returned from the school.

On the way back from the school, we talked about the problems of the schools we had discussed. I reflected upon the conditions in my school in London. How many decades or centuries will it take for these schools to have similar facilities as of the schools in London? However, it was impressive that these schools were making contributions towards educational development and the students doing their best in such a poor condition, too.

We reached the marketplace. 'Let's have a cup of tea', said dad. He took me to a restaurant where we bumped into two of his childhood friends. He introduced me to them, placed an order for tea and started chatting with his friends. I took out my notebook, checked and wrote down the key points, and enjoyed the tea.

When we reached home, it was already four in the afternoon. We had our afternoon meal ready, which I took, and I sat to discuss further about the school support project with dad. 'We have to raise around two thousand four hundred pounds for both schools. Will it be possible to raise that much from my exhibition?', I asked dad.

'If the exhibition goes well, I think, that could be raised. But don't worry my son, if any shortfall I will help you to meet your target from my friend circle, too. I will definitely be able to raise fund for such a good cause.' I felt assured.

I was incredibly happy as a nice initiative was planned. I was also quite sure that the required amount of funds would be raised from the exhibition. Last year, one of my teachers organised an event in the school to raise funds for a similar charitable purpose and he raised around two thousand and two hundred pounds. There was no reason that my event would not be able to raise two thousand four hundred pounds. All the students, their parents and teachers would help me. Assurances from my dad were just a backup plan.

CHAPTER 21

Time was flying by. It had already been a week since I arrived in the village. The daily activities included walking around the village, visiting relatives and attending lunches or dinner receptions for us. I was so in tune with the village circumstances that I forgot that I had been in the village for just a week and had to return to London after a couple of weeks. Instead, I had a feeling that I had belonged to and had lived there for ever.

It was my second Saturday in the village. We had a plan that day to visit *Siddhakali*, a temple of a goddess. I was waiting for my friends after my breakfast. I had already got ready my notebook, pen and camera. My friends arrived one after another.

Our group entered the main cluster of the settlement starting from the playground above our house. We walked from the lower end to the upper end of that beautiful settlement talking to each other, greeting local people we met on the way and answering their questions about my education and London. I was no more a stranger to the village people. Whoever I had not met yet, asked who I was, whose son or grandson and upon getting my reply, they started behaving as if I were their own child. I compared this social practice with the social lifestyle in London. Unknown people cannot be expected in London to behave towards a newcomer like in this village. People in London are more independent, they are happy with their personal life and do not care or pay attention to any new people. Sometimes, they do get together with friends and enjoy themselves but there is no such community heartiness towards a newcomer. I appreciated the friendliness of these people and this village.

We reached a hilltop up from the village cluster where there was a traditional rest point called *Ghumaunechautaro* (a trekkers' rest point). The hilltop had a nice panoramic view. It was heavenly, I could see further than I had been able to see from *Gadhidanda* the previous week. I was mesmerised by such a beautiful landscape. Why did my parents move to London leaving such a heaven?

We moved ahead and reached a place called *Bhyagutedhunga* (Frog Stone). A big stone which looked exactly like a frog. Incredible, one after another astonishing things and views! My friends picked up the leaves of mug wort and offered to the frog stone. They asked me to do the same. There was a big pile up of the mug wort leaves offered by other passers-by.

'Why is a leaf of mug wort offered instead of a flower? Is it because it is available around?' I wanted to know the reason behind this practice.

Sirjana replied, 'It is not because mug wort is easily available. It's a tradition since long long ago. People say that there is an interesting story behind it. Our parents or grandparents may know the story.'

My grandma was a living book of folklores. I felt assured that she would tell me.

We walked for a further fifteen minutes and reached the temple of the goddess *Siddhkali*. Sweta, Rachana and Sirjana had carried flowers, fruits and other bits from home to offer in the temple enough for all of us. We carried our share individually from outside the temple. There was a sign at the door of the temple that no shoes and leather items were allowed into the temple.

So, we took off our shoes and leather belts and made three clockwise circles of the temple before entering. One by one, we offered flowers and fruits and greeted the goddess by putting our forehead on her feet. There was a designated spot to light the candles and incense sticks in the front yard of the temple close to the door. When we came out of the temple, we lit our candles and incense sticks, we went back to the door and greeted the goddess again.

While I was putting my shoes back on, I asked my friends, 'What is the history of this temple? When was it built? Do you know anything about it?'

Sachin spoke, 'Yes, I know something. The story of this temple is related to Lord *Shiva* and Goddess *Satidevi*. I'll tell you what I know.' By the time he started telling the story, we had already started walking back home. I was keen to learn about such legendary stories.

Sachin began, 'According to the legend, long ago in prehistoric times called *Satyayug*, Goddess *Satidevi* was the first wife of Lord *Shiva*. Love between them was very deep. One day, Goddess *Satidevi* passed away. Because of the death of his wife, Lord *Shiva* had

133

gone mad and started wandering the earth carrying her dead body on his shoulders for many days. After some days, organs from the dead body of Goddess *Satidevi* started falling off. First, here at *Siddhakali*, her right eye fell off. Since then, people started worshipping the goddess establishing a temple and gave its name to be *Siddhakali*. Then her left eye fell off in a place called *Bhojpur* where there is also another *Siddhakali* temple. Her teeth fell off in a small hilltop called *Vijayapur* close to the city of *Dharan*, three days walk from here, and there is the temple of *Dantakali* (tooth goddess). Lord *Shiva* reached Kathmandu valley where the bum of Goddess *Satidevi* fell off and there is a temple of her called *Guhyeshwari*. In this way, it's the people's belief that each place where an organ of goddess *Satidevi* was fallen off, there is a temple of her. Even after the whole dead body had disappeared, Lord *Shiva* still mourned *Satidevi*. Then, all of the gods came down on the earth, and told him that the Goddess *Satidevi* had been reborn as *Parvati*, daughter of the Mountain King; they asked him to marry her again and live with her as *Shiva-Parvati*. Lord *Shiva* is believed to have his *Third Eye* in the middle of his forehead which he opens either to see the whole universe from his location or to blow fire for any destruction he thinks necessary. Hearing the gods, Lord *Shiva* opened and looked through his *Third Eye* and saw that the gods were right. This soothed him and he later married Goddess *Parvati*.

Sachin ended the story saying, 'People say that we had the original eye in the temple for long time, but that now we have is a duplicate one. Why is there a duplicate, not the original one? I've got no clue. People do not always get a chance to see even the duplicate one as it is shown only on a special occasion not always. So, we also did not see it. As it is the first place that Goddess *Satidevi's* organ fell off, it is believed that anyone who comes and prays at this temple, their wish is fulfilled soon. So, Robin, if you have any wish, it will be fulfilled soon.'

'The only wish I've right now is all about the success of my proposed exhibition for the school support project. May this wish be fulfilled.' My friends already knew about the project.

My friends wanted to know about temples in London. I told them that there are many Hindu temples in London although they are without such mythical history. I've visited four or five of them a number of times each along with my parents. I mentioned that recently the Nepalese community had established a temple called *Pashupatinath* with a Nepalese priest, in South East London.

Back at home, after we had our afternoon meal, we were in front of grandma for her stories. I wanted to hear from her the story about the Frog Stone first I had visited today and asked her, 'Please tell us the story of the Frog Stone. My friends told me that it is very much interesting'.

CHAPTER 22

Grandma, in her usual fashion of telling stories, started with the background, 'The Frog Stone you visited this morning is the female one. There is another exactly same looking Frog Stone on the top of the next mountain called *Madi* across the river, which is the male one. These two Frog Stones look out to each other. We offer them mug wort leaves.'

'Why there is a tradition of offering mug wort leaves instead of flowers?' I asked.

'I'll tell you that in the story.' She was still describing the background. 'It is believed that these two Frog Stones were the real frogs originally. They lived in a lake called *Sabhapokhari*. *Sabhapokhari* is the origin of the river *Sabha* and, hence, the river has got its name. *Sabhapokhari* is an exceptionally beautiful lake that is located to the north from our village and to the south from the mount *Makalu*. The lake is so beautiful that anyone who visits it are mesmerised by its beauty.'

'I've been there twice. It takes three to four days on foot to reach there from our village. People who can walk quicker can reach there in three days. Women and children reach there in four days. It even takes five days for the elderly people. I was young on my first visit and it took four days to reach there. I visited second time when I was older and took five days. There are two ways to go there, via a place called *Barhabise* or via the place called *Guphapokhari*. I went via *Barhabise* both times.' Grandma withheld the story of Frog Stone and started describing memories of her trips to *Sabhapokhari*.

'We had to carry enough food to last our travel to and from *Sabhapokhari*. We had to carry all necessary cooking pots and utensils, too. We travelled through different villages called *Khandbari*, *Barhabise*, *Bhangkharka*, *Mangmaya*, *Mangsima*, *Khongrana* and finally reached *Sabhapokhari*. You know, we have a tradition of providing shelter over night for the people who arrive in the evening and, so, we did not have any problems getting shelter in the villages on the way. However, we had to spend nights in the rock shelters, too, before we reached *Sabhapokhari*. One of those rock shelters is called *Ghopteodar*, which is large enough to accommodate a large group. Just before that rock shelter, there is a valley. The local people said that *Sokpas* used frequently to come and play in the valley before.'

Grandma was describing about her journey to *Sabhapokhari* in every detail. Suddenly, she mentioned about *Sokpas*, which was a completely new thing to me. In my curiosity I broke my silence and asked, 'What is a *Sokpa*, grandma?'

'I don't know much about it. People say that they are human like creatures but wild and live in a snowy region. They are also called Snowmen. Your dad may know more about it, ask him. Instead, the local people had told a story about a *Sokpa*, that I'll tell you.'

I was so fascinated by the description that I asked her to pause for a while, went to see dad who was having a chat with uncle and aunt and asked him to describe the *Sopkas* to me.

'In the local language, people call the wild human like creature a *Sokpa*. Likewise, Snowmen or *Yetis* are also called *Sokpa*. You might have heard about the *Yeti*, haven't you? The word *Yeti* is derived from Tibetan word *Yache*, which means the rock bear. Over time, *Yache* has been mispronounced as *Yeti*. People believe that *Yeti* live in the Himalayas in rocky habitat, and they look like between humans and big apes. When you have time later, study about *Yeti* online or from the books written about *Yeti* to learn more. By the way, your youngest uncle has written a story book entitled 'On the Lap of Yeti' in three volumes. I will ask him to send them for you and read them, too. Is that okay, my son?' Dad wanted to close the conversation on this topic.

'Yes, I've got an interesting topic to research.' I made up my mind and went back in front of grandma and took my seat for her stories.

CHAPTER 23

When I came back and took my seat in front of grandma, she touched my lips with her loving fingers and kissed her finger as her gesture to express her love to me.

'Now, let me tell you the story about a *Sokpa* I heard from the local people that I mentioned a while ago. Once upon a time, there was a man who owned a herd of Yaks, a kind of Himalayan cow. He used to keep his Yaks in a shed made with local bamboo culms and branches. His cow shed was at a lonely place in a distance from his house up on the hill. It was out of sight of the people unless someone came to visit personally. His routine jobs were to clean up the shed, herd his Yaks, milk them, make milk products and so on. He used to milk his cows twice a day, in the morning and in the evening. Once the milk products were ready, he used to take them to his house and his wife to the neighbouring villages for exchanging them with the cereals. They did not have land to grow food grains and it was the only source of earning for their livelihood.'

The man was troubled by a giant *Sokpa* every day in the evening since a couple of days. The *Sokpa* did not harm him personally but used to copy him by milking his cows but on the open ground without having milking bucket and at the end losing milk every day for him. He had to get rid of the *Sokpa*. But how could he do that? No idea was forming in his mind. Should he scare him away? But, the *Sokpa* was big and scary himself – around seven feet tall a robust body covered by white hair, with abnormally long hands and thick feet. He wondered if he should ask his villagers to help him chase the creature away. No, he did not like this idea. He had heard how *Sokpas* were harmless creatures and kind towards humans. He had also heard many stories about how *Sokpas* had helped people. Then, it occurred to him that the *Sokpa* might be willing to help him and had been trying to impress by copying him. He decided to find out.

He got a fire ready outside the shed and placed a utensil on it to boil milk. He also got ready two milking buckets one for himself and the other one for the *Sokpa*. Then, he waited for the *Sokpa* to come over. After a while, the *Sokpa* came over close to the cow shed as usual. The man pretended as if he had not noticed him. He took his milking bucket and milked one of his cows. The *Sokpa* immediately copied him, picked up another milking bucket and milked another cow. After finishing milking a cow, the man poured the milk into the pot and moved away from the fire. The *Sokpa* copied him. He poured the milk into the pot and moved away from the fire. The man and the *Sokpa* continued to milk all cows one after another and poured the milk into the pot on the fire. Excellent! The man was deeply satisfied milk was not being lost. Now, he wondered if he could teach the *Sokpa* more jobs. But he had to do it all by showing experimentally because he couldn't communicate with the *Sokpa.*

The man lit another fire in the fireplace to boil milk, stirred the milk with a spoon and stood at one side waiting for the *Sokpa* to copy. The *Sokpa* had watched it keenly and started stirring the milk. They did it turn by turn until the milk was boiled. After this the *Sopka* did this daily. Sometimes, the *Sokpa* would milk all his cows and pour the milk in the pot for boiling. The man taught the *Sopka* how to light a fire safely and how to clean his cowshed. The *Sokpa* helped him every day and he was happy. Their friendship deepened. They started sitting close to each other and sometimes even huddled. They started communicating to each other using body languages, gestures and objects.

One day, when the *Sokpa* arrived in the evening, he did not see the man outside the shed waiting for him. He was worried. The man had fallen ill, and he had high temperature. He had not been able to get up from his bed. The *Sokpa* went into the shed, for the first time, and found the man lying on the bed. Seeing him on the bed lying, he knew that the man was not feeling well. He went close to him and put his hand on his forehead. He comforted the man and told him, by his gesture, to wait and went out of the shed.

Soon, the *Sokpa* came back with some medicinal herbs in his hands. He made some drops and dripped into the man's mouth. From the first drop, he started feeling better. It took only two days for the man to get well completely. The *Sokpa's* herbs were so effective. He not only cured the illness of the man but also taught him about many medicinal plants that were found in the region. The man first learnt that the *Sokpa* had used a typical Himalayan medicinal plant's leaves called *Bainsh* in local language (Willow in English) for the treatment of his fever. Then he gradually learnt about more medicinal plants over time. The region is rich in medicinal plants.

The *Sokpa* had used a practical method of teaching him. To learn more, the man would go to the villages to find patients. The *Sokpa* would then take him to find appropriate plants for the treatment of that illness. Overtime he learnt about many medicinal herbs and treated many ill people. He became a famous traditional and natural healer in his and neighbouring villages. He went on to educate many others and spread the knowledge. Even today, people believe that knowledge about the medicinal plants in the region was originated from the *Sokpas.*

The story of friendship between a man and a *Sokpa* has been told from generation to generation. People also had a song about this friendship which they sang at festive occasions as a 'Song of Friendship'. It may still exist among only a few people in the remote areas, but I am not sure.

'This was the story I heard from the local people about the *Sokpa.* Did you like it, my dear?' Grandma asked.

'Wow! Song of Friendship! It is really interesting.' I replied.

CHAPTER 24

After the *Sokpa*'s story, grandma continued to describe her journey, 'The trail after the rock shelter called *Ghopteodar* was exceedingly difficult and steep. There were mainly two trails called *Selele* and *Phelele* on the rocky surface. They were so steep that it seemed as if your nose would hit the ground when climbing up; so steep that it felt as if we would fall down to the bottom of the hill if we slipped while walking down. But, may be the rock had been eroded by frost or snow, the surface was coarse and not slippery at all. How strange! Our feet stuck firmly when we took our steps. In this way, walking up and down all those steep trails, climbing mountains and several crossings, we finally reached *Sabhapokhari*. It was amazing! How pleasant was *Sabhapokhari* and its surrounding! When reached there, I forgot all the difficult trails, all the ups and downs and my tiredness.' Her eyes shined when she recalled her exciting journey. When she was describing it, she asked us time to time if we were interested. We nodded our heads every time she asked to express our interest.

'Several kinds of rhododendron are found all over the hills surrounding *Sabhapokhari* – red, white, purple, pink and so many other colours. You know, people say there are twenty-five different colour rhododendrons found in the surroundings of *Sabhapokhari*. In the surrounding forests there are also found different birds and wild animals such as *Danfe* (Nepal's national bird) and *Munal* (both belong to wild pheasant family) and *Ghoral* and *Chittal* (both are like deer or goat). In such a beautiful place, the lake itself was so eye-catching. There is a small island at the middle of the lake. If you see it from a height, the clear water surrounding the island looks like a big bangle of silver. As if God had decorated the beauty of this part of the earth with jewellery. The water is so clean and clear that you feel you can see the bottom of the lake. There is not a single piece of leaf or grass in the lake. People say that if any leaves or pieces of grass fall off into the water, birds come to the lake and use their beaks to remove the pieces and take them out of the lake. The water of the lake is not only clean and clear but also regarded as a sacred water like *Gangajal* (water from the river *Ganges* in India) in Hindu Religion. It is believed that if anybody worships in the temple located by the lake at one corner of the hill after taking a bath in the lake, their wish is fulfilled, and good fortune comes to their family and children. If a couple, who want children but are not having any luck, if they take a bath together in the lake and worship in the temple wishing children, they will have one soon.', Having said this, grandma paused for a while.

She cleared her throat and continued speaking, 'There is a priest who offers daily worshipping of Lord *Shiva* and the *Goddess Parvati*. Further away from the temple, there is a *Buddhist* monastery and a place for meditation. It is believed that there is plenty of divine power accumulated in the surrounding of the lake. Therefore, in the season the snow melts, many Hindu Saints and Buddhist Monks live there for three months in meditation. So, you can say, *Sabhapokhari* is the meeting point of Hindus and Buddhists.

'Now, I'll tell you the history behind the name *Sabhapokhari* that how such a sacred pilgrimage place got its name.'

Grandma gave us an insight of the historical background after describing its present situation. 'A long ago in prehistoric age called *Dwaparyug*, the Great

Saint *Vyas* organised a conference of many saints in *Sabhapokhari* to discuss and perform a *Yagya* (a Hindu ritual in front of a sacred fire often with chanting sacred verses called *mantras*) for the welfare of humankind. They built a stage for performing the *Yagya* on the island at the middle of the lake and prayed to gods to take part in the meeting, too. Being pleased from the *Yagya* of the saints, gods also landed on the place and participated in the meeting. *Sabha* in local language means meeting and *Pokhari* means a pond (lake). Thus, the lake, where a meeting of the gods and the saints took place, got its name to be Meeting Pond (*Sabha Pokhari*)'.

CHAPTER 25

'Now, let me come to the story of *Sabhapokhari* and the Frog Stone.' Finally, she started the main story of Frog Stone, which I was keen to hear. The story she told flows like this.

Once upon a time, in the prehistoric era called *Satyayug*, the lake was the habitat of giant frogs, where they had their own Kingdom. The King and his subjects were all living there happily. They had no illness, pain or sorrow. They were blessed by God. They also had spiritual power. They never harmed anybody. They had all the wealth and power they needed. If enemies attacked them, they used to fight by being organised, the King and his subjects all fought together and defeated their enemies in every battle. Mutual love and respect among the frogs were their source of power. The love between the King and the Queen was an example for all the frogs of the lake. The subject frogs used to sing the love story of the King and the Queen in their own language.

The queen frog was the most beautiful female frog within the frog race on the whole earth. The King and the Prince frogs of other kingdoms had also wished to marry the Queen frog but could not get the chance. The love story of the King and the Queen frog is interesting. The parental home of the Queen frog was in another lake called *Gosainkunda*, on a hilly region towards west direction from *Sabhapokhari*. When she grew up to the age of marriage, her father, the King of the *Gosainkunda* lake's frog kingdom, announced a ceremony for her to select her partner and invited Kings and Princes of the frog kingdoms from all over the world. According to the customs, daughter would select her would-be husband from among those present in the ceremony. In the ceremony, the frog Kings and Princes had come to attend from *Phewa, Rupa, Vegnas, Rara, Phoksundo* and *Mansarobar* lakes and, obviously, the King frog from *Sabhapokhari*. Also present in the ceremony were the frog Kings and Princes from many other small or big lakes or ponds and the seas. Among them all, the King frog of *Sabhapokhari* was the most attractive and handsome. The Princess selected him, put a garland on his neck and they got married.

To take part in the ceremony, there was also a powerful demon frog that came from far away. He desperately wanted to marry the Princess frog. When he was not selected, he considered abducting her forcefully from the King frog of *Sabhapokhari*. He planned and attacked *Sabhapokhari* two times with the purpose of abducting the Queen frog. In the first battle, the demon frog was defeated badly and saved his life by running away from the battlefield. Many frogs of his force were killed in the battle. But the demon frog was not someone who accepted defeat. He knew that he would not be able to defeat the frogs of the *Sabhapokhari* and decided to go for a meditation to pray Lord *Shiva* to be blessed with powers.

The demon frog undertook a long hard meditation not even having food and water for a long time and prayed.

 Lord *Shiva* was pleased with his meditation and prayer, appeared in front of him and said,

'I'm pleased with your prayer frog King. I am here to bless you. Tell me, what blessing you want from me.'

The demon frog was happy that Lord *Shiva* was pleased, appeared in front of him and asked for his blessings. This was the moment he had waited for going through all those hard meditation and prayers. Then he requested Lord *Shiva* to fulfil his wish, 'God, please make me the most powerful frog in this world so that no other frog can defeat me. Please also provide me with all necessary weapons to be the most powerful.'

'I bless you, your wish will be fulfilled', Lord *Shiva* replied, provided him with water, wind and fire weapons then disappeared. After being blessed by Lord *Shiva* along with the weapons, the demon frog planned a second attack over *Sabhapokhari* and organised his big force. This time, he was assured that he would defeat the frog King of *Sabhapokhari* and seize the frog beauty from him.

A few days later, the demon frog attacked the frogs in *Sabhpokhari* for a second time with his huge force. This time he was more powerful. He used the weapons he was blessed with by Lord *Shiva*. He used a water weapon to create strong waves in the lake and pushed the frogs off from the water high into the air; then he used a wind weapon to blow them out from the lake on to the land; and, he used his fire weapon to burn them up. The frogs in the lake did have water, wind and fire armours and used them to protect themselves and they fought with much bravery. But with the blessings of Lord *Shiva*, the demon frog was much more powerful than them. The frog King did not have enough power to defeat him. Soon, all the frogs of *Sabhapokhari* were killed. The frog King was seriously injured, he had wounds all over his body. The Queen frog also fought with bravery alongside the King frog and she was wounded, too. When the King and the Queen frogs realised their defeat, they decided to keep alive their love until their last breath and using all their spiritual powers, they took a long jump together from the lake towards the south.

Having seen the terrible scenario of destructing the whole world of peace loving and harmless frogs in *Sabhapokhari* by the demon frog, Goddess *Parvati* became furious and asked Lord *Shiva*, 'Why did you bless the destructive demon with such power and weapons? Now, please finish him off.'

Lord *Shiva* replied her, 'I'm bound by the divine rules to bless the devotees if their prayer is successful. But I did not think that he would misuse my blessings in this way. Because I have blessed him, I cannot take it back myself. Now, whatever needs to be done, you must do. The least I can do is that I can provide you with all my powers, too.'

The angry goddess appeared at the *Sabhapokhari* with all her powers and weapons in a violent posture. Lord *Shiva* also appeared behind her on the spot. The furious goddess told the demon frog, 'Hey, wicked demon, you have committed an unforgivable sin by destroying these peace-loving frogs. Now, I'll finish you off.'

Seeing such a violent posture of the goddess, the demon frog was frightened and requested Lord *Shiva* to protect him from her. Lord *Shiva* replied him, 'Look demon frog, you misused my blessings to commit such a sin. I did not bless you for such an act. Although I cannot take my blessings back from you, I can't come forward to protect you, too. On top of that, the goddess has already taken my powers with her and I cannot do anything even if I wanted to. Now, be ready to be punished by the goddess for your sin.' The goddess had already taken up all water, wind and fire powers and all the other divine powers with her. Then the almighty goddess in no time finished off the demon frog and all his force. Because the almighty goddess *Parvati* and Lord *Shiva* had appeared together in that place, people, when they learnt about the incident, started worshipping both in that place establishing their temples afterwards.

It is believed that plenty of spiritual power was accumulated in the *Sabhapokhari* region because the almighty goddess had appeared there with divine powers and, therefore, the great Saint *Vyas* had performed a *Yagya* in participation of many saints and even the gods. It is also believed that Lord *Buddha*, later, knowing the facts about the high spiritual powers in the region, came to the place along with his many disciples and had his meditation there for several months. The local people believe that every year many Hindu saints and Buddhist monks come to the place and meditate for this reason.

CHAPTER 26

'I'd told you earlier that the injured King and Queen frogs took a long jump from the lake towards the south together to keep their love alive until their last breath after being defeated by the demon frog, do you remember?' Grandma proceeded with her story.

'Yes, we do.' We replied.

'When the King and the Queen frogs jumped towards the south with their wounded bodies, the Queen frog landed on the hilltop above our village, *Chainpur*. When landed, she died and instantly turned into the Frog Stone, that is what we have today. The King frog landed on the hilltop of next mountain called *Madi* inside a forest. He turned round to look for the Queen frog and saw that she had already died and turned into a stone. He could not bear the pain of death of his love, he also died then and there looking towards the Queen and turned instantly into the Frog Stone, too. Thus, as I said earlier, these two Frog Stones look out at each other across the two hilltops.' Grandma was reaching the climax of the story. We were listening to her spellbound with rapture.

'Because they died having wounds all over their bodies, people started offering them leaves of mug wort, a plant traditionally being used to apply on the wounds as medicine, with their good intentions that it would relieve them from their pain. The same tradition is followed until today. Now, you know why people offer the leaves of mug wort instead of flowers to the Frog Stone. It's a common belief of the local people that people who go and offer mug wort leaves to the Frog Stone, they will get more love from the people around them. If they are children, they are showered by love from their parents and other elders; if they are love birds, their love will be successful; and, if they are a married couple, they will be successful in their married life. Hence, the Frog Stones since unknown time have been offered the leaves of mug wort plant.' Grandma completed her story, and said, 'to the listeners ….' and paused herself leaving the concluding verse for us to tell.

Then we pronounced the verse together.
To the listeners, gold's garland
To the teller, flower's garland

May this story go direct to the god's land.

CHAPTER 27

I wanted to hear more stories and asked her to tell more equally interesting ones.

Instead of starting the story straightaway, she called me to go closer to her and I went. She held my cheeks by her both hands and kissed my forehead and said, 'my prince'. Then I went back and took my seat with my friends.

'Tiger's skin on the waist, snake's garland on the neck …. (a verse dedicated to Lord *Shiva*). It was her speciality to use different methods to draw attention of the listeners before starting a story. She sang this verse at the start and explained the importance of snakes linking them with different gods, 'A snake is an ornament Lord *Shiva* has on his neck. Lord *Vishnu* sleeps on the snake bed. When Lord *Krishna* was born, his father took him to another place from his birthplace to save him from a devil. While carrying him, they had to cross a big river. While crossing the river, a giant snake became an umbrella for them. People say that there is a separate snake kingdom and all the snakes come out to the human world from their world. The snakes in their kingdom have an uncountable wealth of jewels, diamonds and valuable pearls. If the snake gods are pleased with people, they bless them with loads of wealth. Therefore, to please the snake gods, we have a tradition of worshipping snakes once a year on a special day called *Nagpanchami* (Snake Day) which falls on the fifth day of bright half of the month of *Shrawan* (July/August) according to the Lunar calendar of the *Hindus*.'

'Although there is such religious belief, people are frightened if they see snakes. I also get frightened very much if I see a snake. Are you also scared of snakes?' Grandma suddenly asked.

'Yes, we are.' We replied.

'There are many types of snakes around us, green snakes, rat snakes, golden snakes, cobra snakes and many more. They are of different colours and some get their names from their colours, too. But you know, not all snakes are poisonous. Nothing happens if a non-poisonous snake bites. But many people die due to the fear of a snake bite. Do you want to hear a joke that a man died with fear when he knew that he was bitten by a snake even though the snake was non-poisonous?'

'Of course, we want to hear it. Please tell us.'

'You know that houses in the villages have mostly thatched roofs. Those thatched roofs need to be repaired every one or two years.' Grandma gave a background for the joke and continued her story, 'a man in a village got a labourer to repair the roof of his house. You might know that the thatch on the roof is fastened with bamboo strings. While the work man was fastening the thatch on the top ridge of the roof with bamboo strings, one of his fingers was pierced by something and he started bleeding. He simply thought that the bamboo string pierced his finger, wiped the blood off and continued working. Again, the following year, the house owner called the same man to repair his roof. After one year, the labourer found a skeleton of a snake fastened with a bamboo string exactly at the same spot where the previous year his finger was pierced and was bleeding. Oh no, was I bitten by a snake last year? He got frightened and his whole body turned cold with fear. He left the job, got down from the roof and told other people that he was bitten by a snake the previous year. After a while, because of the fear of snake bite, the man died.

'The man died, only because of fear, one year after he was bitten by a non-poisonous snake.' Grandma commented and laughed loudly. When she laughed, her toothless mouth was fully opened, and the waves of her laughter moved through her numerous wrinkles on her face. We also could not stop our laughter and joined grandma to laugh loudly. Because of the laughter, we had tears in our eyes which we wiped off after we stopped laughing.

'Did you know, how much people are frightened of a snake?' Grandma preceded her story after she stopped laughing. 'I also get scared. I start shaking with fear if I see a snake. Can you imagine? I, such a fearful woman, was once wrapped by a big snake. Oh my god! You can imagine my reaction at that moment. It still scares me, and my hair stands on end if I remember that moment. Let me tell you the incident. Will you be scared?'

'No, we won't be. Please tell us', we replied. I made my heart strong and, hopefully, my friends did the same.

'This was an incident that happened in the *Terai*, the plain region of our country; many years back, your dad was not even born. In those days, we had a farmland and a house in the *Terai*, too. We had to go there during cultivating and harvesting times every year. Mostly, your grandpa used to go alone. I'd heard that many snakes would be found in the *Terai* and for this reason, I did not want to go. But what could I do? Sometimes I could not avoid from going there. In the year the incident happened, I had accompanied your grandpa and was in our *Terai* farmhouse.' She gave a brief background.

'Our farmhouse along the front and backyards was surrounded by a wooden fence. To the front of the house, the fence was adjoined to a main public footpath for the local people to go to the town centre. I used to go to the town centre for shopping kitchen needs once or twice a week. It was two miles away from the village. One day, I and a neighbour were going to the town centre together. The woman came and we left our house. As I said, outside our house, there was our wooden fence on one side of the footpath, but the other side of the footpath was an open farmland. It was a rainy season and the edge of the footpath towards the farmland was all covered by long grass.' She described the surroundings.

Then she described the incident. 'We had just got out of our compound gate and walked eight or ten steps, when we saw a big golden snake, of almost our arm's size in diameter, coming out from the grass and standing straight up flattening its head. The snake stood up to the level to our stomachs. It was remarkably close to us. I felt like I had stopped breathing. My hands and legs started shaking. In fact, my whole body and heart was shaking. It was not clear whether I or my friend would be the victim of the snake's bite. There were three men walking some twenty to twenty-five steps behind us. When they saw a big snake standing up in front of us and ready to bite, they stopped on the spot. They had thought one of us two women would be finished.'

'What to do? What not to do? I could not think. I felt like my mind was empty. Unknowingly, I closed my eyes and started praying. Hey god, please protect us. My children are still small. If I die, they will suffer a lot. While I was praying to god with my eyes closed, the snake started wrapping around me. The snake, starting from my legs, wrapped up my whole body, had reached above my head and had flattened its head like an umbrella.'

'I'd heard that the snakes are cold. That is true. I felt very cold on parts of my body where my clothes had not covered. I closed my eyes more tightly and started praying, hey snake god or goddess! I have never harmed any snake. Please do not harm me, too, and leave me.'

'Don't be afraid of me, dear. I am not here to harm you but to bless you. I am a snake goddess. Open your eyes and look at me.' I could not believe my ears to hear these words. With a great surprise, my eyes opened on their own. I was stunned by what I saw when   my eyes

opened. In front of me, there was really a snake goddess, a beautiful woman with golden hair tresses, a golden dress full of different jewellery. Amazingly, she had a cucumber-seed-sized object on her forehead between but just above her eyebrows flashing blue, red and yellow coloured lights turn by turn and that was her serpent jewel. She had a thick but short maroon coloured line painted upright on her forehead just above her serpent jewel. I looked around me. I found my friend, the three men behind us, plants, wind and time everything stood still, suspended. 'I've come here to take you to our palace as sent by the king snake god to bless you. I will bring you back after completing the blessing ceremony in our palace. Until then, everything will remain suspended at all like this and they will know nothing.' A moment after she said this, I was in the palace of the snake gods and goddesses.

What a mesmerising palace! It was wonderfully decorated and shining with the jewels, pearls, diamonds and many more valuable objects. This was the palace of the King Snake. I found that all the snake gods and goddesses were devotees of Lord *Vishnu*. All of them have exactly same maroon coloured line painted, a sign of Lord *Vishnu's* devotees, on their forehead above their flashing serpent jewels and they all were chanting together melodiously 'Shreeman Narayan, Shreeman Narayan (a verse dedicated to the Lord Vishnu). There was a conference of the snake gods and goddesses going on. All had shining costumes and jewellery. The King Snake god was seated on a fantastically decorated and shining throne. The name of the King Snake was Sheshnag. He was himself the cushion of Lord Vishnu and, hence, all the snake gods and goddesses were devotees of Lord Vishnu.

When I was taken to the conference hall, the snake king welcomed and blessed me saying, 'I bless you on behalf of all snake gods and goddesses. May you get complete happiness in your life. Your destiny is that your path of devotion to the god is like ours, i.e. devotion to Lord Vishnu. Although you have not followed the path yet, you will do one day. You will become a devotee of Lord Vishnu as a Shreemargi Vaishnav (one of the two main paths of devotion to Lord Vishnu) in the future. Now, you've got our blessings and the snake goddess will take you back to the spot from where you were picked up.' Then they again started chanting 'Shreeman Narayan'.

I cannot say whether it was real or a dream or an illusion. I woke up and returned to normal, wrapped by a snake and praying to the gods with my eyes closed. Meanwhile, I felt that I was being released from the snake wrap and the snake left me. I still had my eyes closed with fear. The men behind us called me. I heard them and, so, I opened my eyes. The snake had already gone but I was still shivering.

The men took us into our house, and they described everything that had happened. One of them was saying, 'Ma'am, don't be frightened anymore. The snake god or goddess had come to bless you. The snake was golden coloured. Did you see it? The snake did not harm you. Instead it wrapped you reaching above your head and provided shelter with its flattened head. You know, that was the way a snake god or goddess blesses you. It is believed that if a snake wraps and leaves anyone, the person receives good fortunes. Wrapping and leaving by a golden snake is even more fortunate. They will start getting more and more wealth. Your family may also see the same good fortune from now onwards. You should not be frightened anymore instead you should be happy that you are blessed by a snake god or goddess. If it had wanted to harm you, it would have bitten you.'

After the man reassured me, my fear vanished, and I felt relieved. I had had also heard that the person wrapped by a snake would be lucky. Not to mention, your grandpa acquired additional farmlands both in the hills and the *Terai* (the southern belt of our country) afterwards. I am not sure, whether it was due to the blessing or his hard work. Nonetheless, other village people who did similar hard work were not able to earn equally. It confirms to me that it had been possible because of the blessing of the snake god.

Grandma concluded her story, 'The news of the incident that I was wrapped by a golden snake spread throughout the village. People started coming in to see me not only from within the village but from the neighbouring villages, too and it continued for many days. That's it. The story ends here. Now what needs to be said at the end of a story, you can conclude yourself.'

Then we chanted together:
To the listeners – gold's garland

To the teller – flower's garland

May this story go direct to the god's land.

Grandma had a unique habit. After speaking for a while or telling a story, she used to keep quiet herself, push her lips into her toothless mouth, pretend as if she was chewing something and then produce a peculiar sound from her throat right at the bottom of her tongue. She did the same thing after telling this story and produced that peculiar sound kraunk, kraunk, kraunk.

CHAPTER 28

Breaking a momentary silence, grandma got prepared to tell another story. She had already decided which one to tell us.

'I told you about the incident that happened with me in the *Terai*. Now I will tell you another incident that happened to me in *Assam*, India. Is that alright, children?'

'Alright, we are eager to listen.' We replied and got ready to listen.

First, as usual, she started giving a brief background of the story, 'In those days, people, mainly men, from our village used to go to *Assam*, *Meghalaya* and *Manipur* in India to earn a better living. Many of them even settled over there permanently. In his thirties, your grandpa also had lived in *Assam* and he had a sugarcane farm and some buffaloes. During that period, he used to come home once or twice a year. I have also been there two or three times with your grandpa and lived there for a couple of months each time. The life was not easy there, though. He had to work hard to make money. But the income was good from the sale of both sugarcane and buffalo milk. With the earnings from *Assam*, your grandpa had been able to buy lands in the *Terai*.

Portraying grandpa's life in *Assam* then she said, 'Your grandpa had taken around two acres of land on lease for sugarcane farming. Likewise, he used to always keep three milking buffaloes. If any buffalo stopped milking, then he used to sell it and buy another milking one in its place. Life was busy over there. Every day from early in the morning, the routine job of taking care of those buffaloes would start. Feeding them, giving them water, cleaning their sheds, taking them for grazing and playing in the pond, milking them twice a day and so on. Your grandpa was so active that he used to wash all three buffaloes with clean water after they had played in the pond before bringing them back home. After bringing them back, he used to rub fresh mustard oil on their whole body, horns and legs. He believed that by doing so the buffaloes would not get any illness. Your grandpa had such a lot of work to do every day and they were milking the buffaloes, mixing that milk in a drum with the milk from previous evening and carrying a drum of milk on his back to take to the collection centre. Your grandpa was always so busy working hard.'

'Now, let me tell you about the sugarcane farming.'

'Sugarcane farming also needed a lot of hard work; preparing land for plantation preparing trenches for irrigation, planting the sugarcane, ensuring regular irrigation, removing weeds; in the harvest time, cutting the sugarcane, preparing bundles by removing ends and dried leaves and taking these to the buyers. There was a lot of work for him from planting to harvesting and selling. It was an all year-round job. However, sugarcane farming was not like buffalo keeping that your grandpa could do everything alone. Instead, he had to get labourers to help with most of the farming jobs. However, he had to supervise the labourers closely.'

'The village where we lived was quite a distance from the town centre. One side of the village was adjoined with one side of a big forest. The forest was a perfect habitat for tigers, bears and wild elephants. There were around forty houses in the village, but they were clustered in one place. All the houses were two storeyed made up of wood with zinc plate roofs. Ground levels were used to keep cattle and people lived on the upper level. There were hand pumps for water and was not a problem of going far to fetch like here in the hills. There was no electricity in the village and had to use kerosene lanterns for light.'

'There was a school in the village running classes up to year group five. Older children had to go to the town centre and used to travel on bicycles to get to their school. At one corner of the village, there was a small police station, where there used to be only five policemen. At another corner, there was a grinding and rice mill operated by diesel as there was no electricity in the village. As it was operated by diesel, the mill used to produce a lot of smoke. A long pipe was erected straight up to pass the smoke. There was a metal pot like a deep bowl fitted upside down on a tripod stand at the top end of the pipe and there was a gap between the metal pot and the end of the pipe. Every time the mill produced the smoke, it would come up to the end of the pipe and hit the metal bowl, by which a sound was produced. The pot was fitted that way with a purpose of producing sound to let people know that the mill was running. The sound was heard everywhere in the village. So, when the mill was running, the mill's sound was heard, puk, puk, puk ....' In this way, grandma presented a clear picture of the village.

CHAPTER 29

After finishing the description of the village, she cleared her throat and continued speaking. 'The village people were hard working and were making a good living from their hard work. They were happy. However, there were always risks and fears and no peace of mind for two reasons. Firstly, the fear of bandits, who used to come to the village to rob their assets. Secondly, the fear of wild animals like tigers, bears and wild elephants, who used to enter the village sometimes. First, I will tell you about the bandits and then about the wild animals.'

'There used to be incidents of bandits attacking the village and robbing their money and jewellery once or twice a year. A group of fifteen to twenty bandits used to come to the village from unknown places carrying guns and other weapons. Then they used to enter every house with their guns positioned and rob money and jewellery whatever the villagers had. Anybody who opposed them was shot dead. When the policemen learnt that the bandits had entered the village, they used to hide themselves, and only come out after the bandits had left the village to start their investigation.'

'But, for the past couple of years, there had been no such incidents of robbery. To protect themselves from robbery, the villagers organised and got permission from the government to keep guns at homes for self-defence. In an incident after the villagers had guns with them, the bandits attacked the village again as before. The villagers fought back in an organised way. When the villagers started fighting the bandits, the policemen also joined them instead of hiding themselves. In the crossfire, four bandits were killed. Seeing a big group of villagers including policemen fighting them, they quickly ran away. After that incident, they did not come back again and there had been no incidents of robbery in the village.'

'In that fight between the villagers and the bandits, two sad incidents had happened. A boy and a girl, both were in their mid-twenties, had come back to their homes that day from the city after completing their education. They both took part in the fight and they fought with bravery. The boy shot dead three bandits one after another. But bad luck! A bullet fired by a bandit hit him and he fell on the ground. With difficulty, he stood up and fired back the bandit who had shot him and was able to shoot him dead, too. After shooting dead the fourth bandit, he fell again and died. Thus, the villagers lost one of their brave sons for ever. On the other hand, the bandits thought that they would not be able to fight any longer and ran away. But more bad luck! While running away, the bandits were able to catch the brave girl, who was bravely fighting alongside the villagers. They abducted her.'

Grandma made the story more interesting and said, 'That girl was not only brave but also clever. While she was being taken away by the bandits, she did not try to escape from them. Instead, she decided to know where the bandits live and plan to finish them off. The bandits had their shelter in a remote place. People who knew about their shelter, would not go there out of fear. When they reached their shelter, the gang leader told her that they had kidnapped her to ask the villagers for a good ransom for her return. If they did not pay money, they would kill her. She shivered with fear and started crying. In fact, she was not afraid and crying but she was pretending it to show them. Then the leader said to his people to get ready their dinner and drinks and bring dinner for the girl as well. Leaving her in a small corner on the one side they gathered in a spacious corner on the other side. They started enjoying their dinner and drinks without paying attention towards her. They thought of her as a helpless poor girl as other girls or boys they had kidnapped previously and would wait for her parents or the villagers to exchange her with their ransom demand. But she was watching them closely. When the gang was busy in eating and drinking, she stood up, went away quietly like a cat moves and escaped from them. She thought, if she would take the same route she had arrived, the bandits might find her if they came looking for her. She was so clever that she took the opposite route and walked fast. When the bandits noticed she had escaped, they indeed did try to find her along the same route she had been brought earlier. So, luckily, they could not find her.'

'The girl walked nonstop and reached a river. There was a village across the river and a town centre a bit further. There was no bridge on the river. She knew how to swim and therefore dived into the river without delay. She crossed the river swimming quickly.' Grandma was telling the story as quickly as flowing water. We were listening to her spellbound.

'After crossing the river, the girl continued to walk fast. Finally, she reached the town centre and went straight to the police station. She described to the police officers all the details of the incident and showed them by drawing a map to where they lived. Listening to her, the police team decided without delay to go and arrest them. Immediately a large team of policemen equipped with guns and set off towards the bandits' shelter place. The girl also accompanied them. The police team reached their shelter and surrounded them. The police force was able to arrest them all. The gang leader of the bandits looked at the girl furiously, but he was not able to do anything as they were all handcuffed.'

'That brave and clever girl became the pride of the village. She was also awarded by the government for her bravery. She joined the police force later and arrested many bandits' gangs. Like this story, I've also heard about the bandits of *Chambal* Cross and the *Jhinjha* village.'

The new context increased my curiosity and asked, 'What is the story of the bandits from the *Chambal* Cross and the *Jhinjha* village, grandma?'

'The *Chambal* Cross is at the bank of the river called *Chambal* somewhere in India. There are numerous small mountains and the crossings in between those mountains which is called the *Chambal* Cross. Groups of bandits have lived in those crossings secretly and they go around to the villages for robbery. I've heard, they are not only involved in robbery but also, they are known for the assassination of people. There was also a woman who was the leader of one of the gangs. I've heard that an Indian movie was made about that woman. If you get a chance, watch that movie then you may have more idea about her. Whereas *Jhinjha* is one of the villages in the *Terai* region of our country, Nepal. The occupation of the people of the entire village used to be robbers, traditionally. They used to do nothing else for their livelihood but robbery. You know, people say that the *Jhinjha's* bandits never robbed their neighbouring villages. They had adopted this as their value. The then king of Nepal heard the story about the *Jhinjha's* bandits. Then the king visited their village to see them and appealed to them give up their occupation of robbery. In return, he offered to resettle them in fertile land somewhere else enough for their livelihood. They accepted the king's offer, gave up robbery permanently and were resettled. Hence, the long story of *Jhinjha's* bandits ended. The story of bandits ends here.' Grandma finished her story about bandits adding some context of bandits from *Chambal Cross* and *Jhinjha Village.*

CHAPTER 30

Although grandma was telling her stories one after another, they all were interesting, and we were keen to listen. After the story of robbery, she started background for the next one.

'I told you earlier that there were two fears in the village, from bandits and the wild animals in *Assam*. I told you about the bandits and now I am telling you about the wild animals. There was a big forest close to the village, one part of which adjoined the village. The forest was the habitat for different wild animals such as tigers, bears, jackals, foxes, monkeys and so on. All of them used to give us trouble from time to time. Among all, tigers, bears and the elephants were the most dangerous.

Tigers used to enter the village and prey on domestic animals. Bears and wild elephants used to enter the sugarcane farm to enjoy its juice. If they were not chased away quickly, they used to destroy the sugarcane farm. The villagers had their own method of pushing them away. Immediately after the villagers knew about their arrival, a big group of the people used to come out of their houses with their drum sets and other instruments and start playing them loudly. When people used to get closer in a large group playing drums and other instruments, the animals used to run away, and they were chased until they went back to the forest. Once it happened, the animals would not come back for some days.'

'I was in *Assam* with your grandpa one year. It was sugarcane harvest season. One day, your grandpa had gone to the sugarcane farmland. I was alone at home. The incident happened in the afternoon. I was collecting paddy I had spread in the sunlight to dry up in the courtyard earlier in the day. Meanwhile, a wild elephant came into the village. Phew! It came closer to me. I started shivering with fear. I ran away through the road in the village to save myself thinking that he would certainly kill me. Other people in the village were also running away. The elephant followed me. When I was running, my foot hit something and I fell on the ground'.

'The elephant caught me, wrapped me in his trunk and threw me hard on the ground. Yeow ... It hurt me so much. I felt like my waist was broken. But suddenly I remembered one thing. I had heard that if an elephant attacks and if you pretend to be dead by  stopping breathing, the elephant will leave and go away. When I remembered this, I closed my eyes, prayed to god, stopped breathing and pretended as if I were dead. I heard that the villagers were saying from a distance that the elephant would kill me. But the elephant did not lift me by his trunk and smash on the ground a second time. Instead, he started rolling me on the ground using his trunk to push. When I was being rolled and my face turned downwards facing the ground, I took a breath secretly every time. I was very smart, weren't I? After rolling me about another ten feet, the elephant stopped and went away leaving me there.' Hearing such a fearful incident happened with grandma, I was also frightened and, my body puffed up.

Her story had not ended yet, 'Seeing the elephant chasing me, one of the villagers had rushed to call your grandpa to the sugarcane farm. When your grandpa heard about the incident, he had thought that he might have already lost his wife and the elephant would have already killed me. He came rushing along with all the labourers to the spot. But, by the time he arrived, the elephant had already gone, and I was sitting on the ground shaking through my whole body. He caught both my arms and got me to stand up. He removed dust from my clothes with his loving hands and took me inside house with his support. He immediately washed my wounds, made some ointment from local medicinal herbs and applied to my wounds. It took several days, a month or more, for me to recover. Thus, I returned right from the mouth of death.'

Grandma completed the story and pronounced the wrap up verse, 'to the listeners. . .' The story telling session was over for that day. It was already evening, and my Aunty let us know that the dinner was ready. 'That's all for today. I'm now feeling tired.' Having said this, grandma stood up from her seat and went to get ready for her dinner. My friends also left to go their homes. I took my dinner and went to my bedroom.

Lying down on the bed, I started recalling everything from the day; the visit to the *Siddhakali* temple and the stories about *Sabhapokhari* lake, *Sokpa*, Frog Stone, snake, bandits and the wild elephant, I recalled everything with vivid details; I made notes of what I needed. I was happy because I'd been given plenty of ideas of places to study such as the natural beauty of *Sabhapokhari* region and other lakes and legends like the *Sokpa* or *Yeti*. I felt proud of my grandma for her stories, her effective methods of telling stories and knowledge she had. All these increased my love and respect towards her. I felt that I was fortunate to have this opportunity to see her.

CHAPTER 31

Three weeks had already elapsed. How fast the time was passing! I wished the time would stop for some time. I wished I could control time in my way. But it goes away on its own way, on its own pace.

We had a plan to visit *Baneshwar* hill that Saturday. I got ready after my breakfast and was awaiting my friends. I did not have to wait for long. Within ten minutes, all my friends arrived. Without any delay, we proceeded for *Baneshwar* hill. At *Daregaundachautaro* (rest point), we stopped and chatted. We started our trek again and reached our destination crossing various places called *Duibare*, the forest of *Khalanga*, *Khatrigaun* and *Arunthan*. On the way, we talked about the villages around, natural landscapes and local cultures and traditions. In between, I asked my friends to allow me to take notes and the photographs.

'What a majestic view! It's incredibly beautiful! So much eye catching! Fabulously fantastic!' These words came out of my mouth with a great amazement without even thinking.

Sachin was right. I had a wider and more beautiful views from the top of the *Baneshwar* hill compared to the views from *Gadhidanda* and *Ghumaunechautaro*. I had a very clear views of the entire *Arun* valley including confluence of two rivers, *Arun* and *Sabha*, a beautiful view of the *Arun* river flowing up like a snake winding through the bottoms of the numerous mountains, the plain land where there is an airport and other many plain cultivated lands, steep terrains and a clear white Himalayan range. I looked at those arresting scenes for quite a while storing them in my mind. I had heard many times from my dad that the *Arun* valley is the lowest valley on the earth and the valley is rich in the biodiversity. I felt very much lucky to see it for myself. I took time to take photographs of the landscapes and made notes in my notebook.

The highest spot of the *Baneshwar* hill is a round shaped peak. Nothing stops the views while viewing from that peak. Below the peak southwards, there is a temple of Lord *Shiva* and further below, a beautiful natural pond. The water in the pond was clean and clear and there were many red fish swimming in the water. What a mesmerising sight! I remembered the

London Aquarium. When I visited it, I had enjoyed it quite a lot. However, the Aquarium was an artificial one whereas that pond and the fish in were all natural.

I discovered that there were also cultural and festive aspects related to the *Baneshwar* hill. My friends mentioned that on one specific festive day in December, many devotees gather at the temple and they perform their religious rituals every year. The devotees bring grain seeds and spread them around the temple. People believe that they will be blessed by the god to have better harvest of the grains by doing such a ritual having been fasted whole day.

'You know Robin, it is really a fun day.' Sirjana started describing another interesting event on the day known as Orange Festival.

She said, 'Actually, you can say the Orange Festival is the festival of children. Traditionally, hundreds of big bamboo baskets of oranges are brought by the people and poured from the top of the hill. The scenario of oranges rolling down on the hill and children running behind them to catch them is so amazing. Hundreds of children run upwards and downwards to catch the rolling oranges. In this fun event, adults also participate. However, adults mainly do the task of pouring down the oranges. People bring the oranges having picked them freshly from their orange gardens. People have a belief that the more oranges are caught by the children the better yield of their orange gardens they will have in the following years. In the recent days, popularity of this festival has increased so much that people who do not have their own orange garden also have started bringing oranges buying from others to participate in this event. There is a quite large gathering of adults as well to observe the fun. Interestingly, some adults are also seen running to collect the rolling oranges.'

'Interesting, what a fun! It sounds like a unique festival. Why is it confined within the local villages? This could be an exceptionally good tourist attraction.' I said. How my friends found my reaction, I don't know, they were smiling looking at me while I was canvassing an imaginary collage of the event in my mind.

CHAPTER 32

We were sitting on the ground in circle when we were talking about the Orange Festival. It was a nice and pleasant weather, sunny and clear. Sirjana was to my left almost huddled. I had clearly noticed that she wanted to come as close to me as she could. It happened since day one when we visited a hilltop. Did she like me? We were too young for it, I thought.

However, Sirjana was gorgeous. She had long and radiant silky hair. Her beautiful eyelashes on her hazel eyes have helped her to stand out of the crowd. A slim body with her thin waist, beautiful nose and thin smiling lips made her look elegant look, this all without any artificial make up. Her smile, her perfect sparkling teeth would mesmerise anyone. It was as if god had taken his time to shape her to perfection. She was a perfect match to the beauty of the nature that I had been observing. When I saw her for the first time, I was stunned, and I could not take my eyes off her. I found myself sneaking glances at her. At the same time, I often found her looking at me. In fact, I noticed that she tried her best to take every opportunity to walk or stand or sit beside me as if she wanted to be near me.

'Guys, let's have a singing session. The weather is beautiful and it's nice to sing in such a pleasant moment. Robin, do you like singing, too?'

It was an unexpected proposal of Sirjana. Other friends supported her instantly. I learnt from them that she was a star in the school with her charming voice - one more wonderful thing about her.

I replied, 'Yes, I do like singing and listening to songs. Singing is my hobby and I enjoy it with a guitar. I have composed a few songs for myself and I enjoy singing them. I equally enjoy listening to Nepalese folk songs.'

'Brilliant, we would love to hear your song. Will you sing one of your own songs for us, Robin?' It was Eashan now.

'Sure. But, let me have some time to remember the lyrics and the music. Until then, you guys sing one song each and at the end, I'll sing my song.' I said.

Then they sang a Nepalese folk song each starting by Eashan and at the end by Sirjana. They sang genuinely nice folk songs. One or two songs were new to me. Not to mention, as described earlier by friends, Sirjana had a voice of an angel. I was so impressed that I even advised her to think about producing her music albums in the future. For this, if needed, she could also join music classes.

It was my turn now. I was feeling a bit odd because I did not have my guitar with me. However, I had to sing without guitar, and I hummed for a second to prepare myself. Then I sang this song, the music of which was composed by myself and the lyrics I had picked up from my dad's unpublished poetry collection book. The song was dedicated to the young generation. They liked it very much as they said after I sang the song.

We're the hope
We're the sight
We're the world
We're the light.

Gaining the wisdom that we need
We shall act for good that we find

Raising high the flag of humanity
We shall do our best for humankind
We've started taking our steps
We've to walk still a long way, though
We have started sharing our thoughts
There is still a lot to say, though.

We're the hope ....

I believe in me, in you, my friends, indeed, in all of us
Having a trust mutually, let's believe in the strength of us
By taking our steps together, we shall reach the goal along
By speaking our minds, we shall sing the friendship song.

We're the hope ....

You extend your helping hand, I extend mine
Let's offer flowers of feelings in our friendship shrine
Should we need, we shall fight together the hardship
And, we shall sing with pride our song of friendship.

We're the hope .....

It was almost two o'clock in the afternoon. We had started feeling hungry. We were sure that our afternoon meal was ready, and we returned home. On the way back, we continued talking about many other interesting topics. My friends asked me more questions about London, and I described some interesting things I knew.

Upon returning home, after our afternoon meal, like on the previous Saturdays, we went in front of grandma to hear stories from her. She told four stories one after another which are saved in my mind never to be erased.

CHAPTER 33

'You may not but your friends may know how many festivals are celebrated in our village.' Grandma was ready for the stories.

'We know some, grandma.' My friends replied.

'I may not know all of them either. However, I'll tell you what I know.' Grandma told,

'You might have seen how beautiful is the *Baneshwor* hill.' And, she asked my friends, 'Did you tell him about the cultural aspects of it and the Orange Festival?'

'Yes, we did. We described all interesting aspects, didn't we Robin?' It was Sirjana who had described earlier very well about the Orange Festival on the hill and spreading grain seeds by the devotees around the temple.

'Well done. I don't need to tell anything about it again. Now, I'll tell you one by one about all the festivals we have in our village as far as I know.' Grandma started opening up her bank of knowledge.

First of all, about *Baishakh Purnima* (the Full Moon Day in May). This day is celebrated by both the Hindus and the Buddhists. The Hindus observe this day simply by fasting for the whole day and worshiping the full moon in the evening. The Buddhists celebrate this day greatly as the Lord *Buddha's* birthday. This was the day when Lord *Buddha* was born in *Lumbini*, Nepal, and achieved his enlightenment and died. We have a local tradition that this day is celebrated together by the Buddhists and the Hindus in a local Buddhist Monastery with the candlelight vigils, preaching *Buddha's* teachings and singing verses of Lord *Buddha* containing peace messages.

CHAPTER 34

There is another day in the same Nepalese month which is Mother's Day. In local language, it is called Seeing Mother Day or Feeding Mother Day. This day every mother is seen by their children giving gifts and offering sweets.

'Mind blowing, Mother's Day here and in London are the same'. I remembered Mother's Day that we celebrate every year in London.

'Do you celebrate Mother's Day in London, too, Robin? Who celebrates it, Nepalese or English People?' Sweta asked.

'Actually, celebrating Mother's Day in London is traditionally a festival of Christians. Observing Mother's Day widely was developed by the middle of the twentieth century but linking it with the long-practiced Mothering Sunday for centuries. Mother's Day is observed in London on Sunday three weeks before the Christian festival of Easter. Therefore, this day falls mostly in March every year. But some years it may go to first Sunday in April. Although it seems it is linked to Christian faith originally, today it is found that the people from all communities whether White, Black, Asians observe this day as a common social event.' I tried to satisfy Sweta's curiosity with the knowledge I had. Grandma was also listening to me attentively.

I further told them additional things about Mother's Day in London I had observed, 'These days, Mother's Day is celebrated so widely and with importance that you can see people preparing for it since couple of weeks in advance. The shops are crowded to buy gifts for their mothers. Different coloured flowers and their bouquets are so nicely displayed in the shops throughout the city that you can feel the whole city is converted into a beautiful flower garden. On Mother's Day, it is so pleasant to see thousands of people going to see their mothers carrying gifts and bouquets. On top of that, there is a practice of cutting cakes at home. Not to mention, sales of gifts, bouquets and cakes would go remarkably high on that occasion. Looking at the high sales of these sort of stuff, there is truth in people's saying that the Mother's Day was promoted in this way by the merchants.'

'So, all over the world there seems to be a tradition of celebrating Mother's Day.' Grandma concluded and moved ahead, 'Our other main festivals include *Gaijatra* (the cow festival), *Hilejatra* (the mud festival), *Dashain*, *Tihar*, seed spreading festival and orange festival, *Sakela* festival of *Kirat* communities and *Waleshwor* and *Rambeni* Fairs. Among these, I will tell about *Waleshwor* cave and a fair there after you visit it next week as you told. Today I will tell you briefly about *Dashain*, *Tihar* and *Rambeni* Fair.'

CHAPTER 35

'Let me tell you about *Rambeni* Fair first and then I'll tell about *Dashain* and Tihar.' She started describing it, 'There is a place called *Rambeni* at the confluence of two rivers called *Piluwa* and *Maya*. Of these two, *Maya* river flows from south to north. A river that flows from south to north is regarded as a sacred river. And for this reason, *Rambeni* confluence is regarded as a sacred place as well. Hence, there is a tradition of organising a fair every year in the month of April in this place and is called *Rambeni* Fair. Thousands of people come to observe this fair every year from different villages, neighbouring and from distant villages, too. Dozens of temporary sheds are made by the vendors to keep shops for the shoppers. We can see a crowd of people at every shop to look, choose and buy items they want. It is very nice to see. I used to go every year to observe the fair until I got too old and unable to walk back and forth.'

'There is a temple of Lord *Ram* and a house built for trekkers to take shelter overnight if needed. These buildings, however, do not date back more than three hundred years or so.' Grandma mentioned a brief history of those infrastructures and said, 'The house for the trekkers and a similar house called *Majorpati* here in our village have almost same architecture. People say that both houses were built at the same time. Long before in the history, *Gorkhali* (Nepalese) force had fought in our village against an attack by the Tibetan force. The Tibetian force was defeated by the Gorkhali force. There was a fort of Gorkhali force on the hilltop of *Gadhidanda*, which you have already visited. A Major of the Gorkhali Army, commander of the force, brought skilled workers from Kathmandu and built the trekker's house and, hence, it got its name after him as *Majorpati* (a *Pati* is like a house). The Army Major also used the same skilled workers to build the trekker's house at *Rambeni*, too, and so both look alike.'

CHAPTER 36

After finishing the story of *Rambeni*, grandma started telling about *Dashain*, 'Long ago in the prehistoric era called *Tretayug*, Lord *Ram* worshipped Goddess *Durga* for nine days and had been able to gain victory over *Rawan*, the devil king of Lanka (now known as Sri Lanka). In remembrance of that, there is a tradition of worshipping Goddess *Durga* for nine days with a provision of *Jamara* (sprouts of maize and barley) during *Dashain*, which falls in the month of September or October. The tenth day of *Dashain* is called *Vijayadashami* (the victorious day) or *Tika*. On the day of *Tika*, senior people of the family or clan or even the community offer *Tika* (raw rice made wet with yoghurt, coloured by a typical red powder and patched on the forehead) along with *Jamara* to the juniors as blessings of the Goddess *Durga*. There is also a provision for the next five days to offer the blessings for them who are unable to visit their seniors on the tenth day.'

'*Dashain* is our great festival. In this occasion, the people who are away from homes come back to celebrate. We have fun during the festival as well.

There are swings hanged on four bamboo poles and wooden wheels in many places. It is really a fun to ride swings, but I am scared of playing on the wheels. It's also pleasant to see group of children waiting for their turns to play on the swings and the wheels.'

While grandma was talking about wooden wheels, I remembered the moments I enjoyed riding the wheels at Woolwich General Gordon Square and Blackheath Fair. I also remembered the London Eye where I had been couples of times. Then I said, 'I enjoy riding on the wheels. I have enjoyed these many times in London. Dad and mom take us to different Fairs. All those Fairs have wheels, slides, caves and other attractions for the children. In every Fair I go; I make sure that I enjoy the wheel. But my sister Greta is scared, and she has never been on one.'

Talking about London made our conversations interesting. After I shared the London's context, grandma said, 'We have swings only at *Dashain* festival and so, it's full of fun for everyone. *Dashain* for us also means cleaning and decorating houses, new clothes, delicious food, swings and seeing relatives. There is a tradition in our village to go every morning for nine days to the temple of goddess *Siddhakali* for worship and to come back home before dawn. Children also go in groups before dawn carrying torches and making noise of their loud talks to wake other up and join them. Your dad used to go every year with his friends when he was a schoolboy. You can ask with him, too. He can tell you how much they would enjoy it.' I had heard from dad many times in London about his visits to the *Siddhakali* temple for nine nights in his groups. Hearing grandma, they all came back fresh in my mind.

CHAPTER 37

'*Tihar* is another great festival of us that comes immediately after *Dashain*.' She continued, '*Tihar* is celebrated for five days. The first day is the Crow's Day followed by the Dog's Day, the Cow's Day, the Oxen's Day and the Brother's Day on second, third, fourth and fifth days, respectively. We worship crows, dogs, cows, oxen on their respective days and sisters worship brothers on the Brother's Day. There is also a culture within one of the ethnic groups called *Newar* where they perform a ritual of worshipping to the self on the fourth day which they call it *Mha: Puja* (worshipping self by oneself). Of those five days in *Tihar*, the third, fourth and fifth days are regarded the most important. On the Cow's Day, the third day, cows are worshipped in the morning, and in the evening many candles are lit and goddess *Laxmi* (goddess of wealth) is worshipped to be blessed with wealth and prosperity of the family by her. On the fifth day, brothers are worshipped by sisters and the brothers give valuable gifts to them in return. Hence, the Brother's Day further strengthens the love between brothers and sisters.'

'Not only this, there are a lot of entertainment happening during the *Tihar* festival.' She gave further description of the festival, 'This festival is also called the festival of lights. During the festival, houses are brightened up with lights. On the third day, everywhere inside and outside of houses candles are lit and the village or even the whole hill is bright with the lights. It's pleasant and peaceful to see such so many lights. Many items of sweets are prepared in every household. On the third day, after worshipping the goddess of wealth, women go into groups and perform a typical cultural act singing and dancing special verses, visiting houses in the village. Such a cultural performance is called *Bhailo* and the groups of performers are rewarded with sweets, fruits and money in return. The verses they sing are all about blessing the family they visit such as: the performers have come to your courtyard to wish your good health, wealth and prosperity; provide us with dresses, sweets and money and in return goddess of wealth will bless your family with wealth and prosperity. Likewise, on the fourth and fifth days, men of the village go into their groups and perform their typical cultural act called *Deusi* and they, too, visit individual houses in the village. They play musical instruments, sing and dance whole night. They sing very typical songs with common lyrics among all: *what a full of lights – deusure* (a rhyme word that represents the cultural act it*self); what is this light of? It's the candlelight – deusure; may we have the fresh sweets – deusure; may goddess of wealth bless your family – deusure* and so on.'

While grandma was describing *deusi* and *bhailo*, I remembered Halloween celebrations in London and compared them to this. I did not think that there was much difference. I shared my experience of Halloween with them, I told them that it is a tradition where mainly children form groups with different masks and face paint, visit houses and collect donations. I have participated in the groups almost every year. Likewise, I described the lights in London during Christmas when the streets are decorated with different shaped lights. They were interested to hear about my experience of Halloween and Christmas.

'I'll tell you two bitter experiences during such an enjoyable festival of *Tihar*.' Grandma now came to the story she wanted to tell us after a long background. I was waiting for this moment.

CHAPTER 38

'There are fireworks during *Tihar*, mainly on the third day. People have all sorts of fireworks from light sounding ones to loud sounding. Children enjoy mainly the sparklers. Likewise, there is open gambling for all five days. I don't like gambling at all. There are incidents that people have lost all their property by gambling during the festival. I am telling you now two incidents related to firework and gambling during the festival. These two incidents happened in different years though. However, both happened on the third day of the festival.' Now she was at the main topics of her stories.

'One year, all the villagers were celebrating the festival of *Tihar*. In the evening on day three, people were busy lighting the candles in every house. Children were enjoying fireworks in their courtyards. Meanwhile, a boy lit up a firework. He had placed the firework on the ground. Unfortunately, it was tilted and gone into the roof of his house instead of going straight up towards the open sky. The thatched roof of his house caught fire and immediately started growing and spreading. Thank God, people were at homes worshipping goddess

Laxmi. Fire… fire… People started shouting. All the neighbours gathered carrying buckets of water and poured the water to put fire out. Some were throwing water from the ground and some had even gone onto the roof. Thus, with collective effort of all neighbours, they were able to put the fire out immediately and did not cause much damage. A delay would have caused the fire to spread to other houses and would not be possible to put out. You can imagine, if the houses which were in a cluster had caught fire, the entire settlement would be burnt up. I still feel Goosebumps throughout my body with fear when I remember the incident.'

Hearing the incident about fire, I remembered the history I had read about the Fire of London. In the seventeenth century, a terrible fire had destroyed one part of London. More than thirteen thousand houses and eighty-seven churches were burnt, which left more than eighty thousand families homeless. Although there are no actual figures available, it is believed that many people were killed by the fire. I shared this historical fact about the London fire with grandma and my friends. However, I also informed them that there are many scientific and technical measures, today, in place to prevent fire and if, by any chance, fire breaks out, there is fire brigade service on standby twenty four seven in many places in the city to immediately control the fire.

At the end, grandma said, 'Do these stories give us lessons? They teach us two things. Firstly, do not play with fire. Small or big, you should always be careful while you are using fire. Fire is both our friend and foe. If the fire is in our control, it is our friend but if the condition is reverse and we are under control of the fire, it's our devastating enemy. Secondly, fire may break out anywhere any time. Keeping in mind the risk that it may occur any time, we should immediately put the fire out before it grows bigger and for that we should be prepared in every possible way.'

Concluding with these important lessons, grandma finished telling the story about the fire and she paused. We were also waiting quietly for her next story. We all were so quiet that you could have heard a pin drop.

CHAPTER 39

Breaking her silence, grandma began another story about a thief, 'This story is all about why gambling makes people thieves. This incident happened on the day of *Laxmipuja,* the third day of the festival. The worshipping room of the goddess *Laxmi* was on the ground floor of our house. In the evening, we were lighting up candles and starting in the worshipping room and then moved to the doors, reception hall and the front yard. All of our family were busy at that moment in the front yard. There is a tradition of offering all our jewellery to the goddess *Laxmi* by placing them by her statue as a gesture that all our wealth belongs to her and she would bless us with more wealth. The ritual of offering our jewellery to the goddess would start immediately after we finished lighting up the candles. So, I went upstairs to bring all our jewellery. I'd carried a kerosene lantern and when I entered the room, I encountered a thief looking for our money and jewellery. In the effort of catching him, I caught his neck scarf and started shouting, thief … thief… When he tried to escape from me, his scarf was on my hand and he reached the window to jump out. I also jumped on him and could catch collar of his shirt, dragged him in and pushed down on the floor. By then, all other family members arrived hearing my shout. All of us caught him tightly, tied his hands behind his back with his own scarf and brought him downstairs in the light.'

'When we could see him in the light, we found that he was known to us, he was from the next village. When we enquired why he was trying to steal our money, he said that he had lost all his money by gambling and had come to steal money or jewellery for gambling. I slapped him two times and said that we would take him to the police. He started crying – Please, I'm not a professional thief. I've never stolen before. This is my first time. Gambling made me thief, too. Please forgive me. Please don't take me to the police. I will be known in my village as a gambler and a thief and will lose all my prestige in society. I've a daughter of marriage age and boys from prestigious families have started coming to see her. If they know that I'm a thief and she is a daughter of a thief, her life will be ruined. Please forgive me for her if not for myself. Then I said – why are you crying now? You should have thought of this before. He promised and said – I swear on my children, I will never gamble and even think about theft in future. Forgive me this time and please do not let other people know about this incident. In fact, you have opened my eyes by catching me on the spot and I owe you for this for life. When he cried, sworn on his children and promised not to do it again, we opened his tied hands and let him go.'

'You see? Gambling ruins life of the people. It may make someone a thief, too. That's why I said earlier, I don't like gambling.' Grandma completed her story singing a stanza of a popular Nepalese folk song and leaving the story ending verse for us to tell, which we did.

'Say no to gambling
Loss of wealth and life crumbling. . .'

CHAPTER 40

'There is a saying 'without knowing what it means, singing *Govinda*' Do you know what it means?' Grandma was starting another story.

'To pretend as knowledgeable without knowledge, am I right grandma?' Nirav replied.

'Not exactly', her short answer.

Now, we had a problem. Me and my friends tried but could not find the right answer. Then I said, 'We did not know. I offer you the village across the river. Now you tell us, what does that mean?'

She laughed loudly and said, 'You should not offer any village, my dear. This is not a riddle. This is a proverb.'

Now I got it. She was initiating a process through proverb to enter another story. I'd read and known many English proverbs but not the Nepalese ones. I knew I would enjoy learning and understanding the meaning of Nepalese proverbs and comparing them with similar English ones. I asked her to explain the meaning of that proverb.

Hearing a request from her lovely grandson, she first comforted my cheeks and started explaining the meaning of the proverb, 'It has a deep meaning. Listen to me. Many people sing the verse *Hare Govinda, Hare Govinda* (a verse dedicated to Lord *Krishna*) and many of them do not understand the meaning of the verse. Whoever sings the verse understanding its meaning, they understand the importance of God and they are blessed by the god. Without understanding the meaning, to sing the verse has no meaning. Likewise, if you read your lessons understanding the meanings, they remain in your mind for long and you can use them for a long time. But if you just learn them without understanding the meaning, they are forgotten quickly. Then what's the point of just learning them?'

Brilliant, what a deep meaning! Really a useful lifelong meaning. I compared this with the English proverb and found closer to – neither rhyme, nor reason. Then I asked her to tell me more proverbs.

'An ox without horns named as pointed horned ox; not working swing makes hundred jerks; a barking dog does not bite; thinking self as a big personality does not make others think. All these proverbs have almost the same meaning. Unknowledgeable stupid people want to show off. Whereas clever and knowledgeable people are patient to listen to others and speak based on their knowledge only. These proverbs are lessons not to speak or try to win favour baselessly.' When she explained the meaning of and lessons from the proverbs, I found them all close to or even exactly same as these English proverbs – empty vessels make much sound; thundering clouds seldom rain; barking dogs seldom bite.

'Let me tell you more sayings. Where the food grain placed, there the greed faced; have wealth have people, no wealth go people; there is no medicines for shamelessness; moustache does not block the mouth to eat; where there is a will, there is a way; consider your throat before swallowing a piece of bone; the work is at one place but going somewhere else; whether the real jungle tiger eats you or not, a tiger in your mind may eat you. There are many more proverbs which are not possible to tell all.' Having said this, she advised me, 'I've heard, one of your uncle's school classmates has written a big volume of Nepalese proverb collection. He lives in Kathmandu. Take his address from your uncle and grab one from him for yourself while you are in Kathmandu on the way back to London.'

Good idea! I thanked and asked her to explain the meanings of the proverbs she just told.

'Where the food grain is placed, there the greed is faced – it indicates a nature of some people that they run only after their benefit. If they do not see any benefit, they turn their back. This kind of people are not trusted in the society. They are also called opportunists and should always be aware of them. Have wealth - have people; no wealth - go people. This talks about the nature of people again. If you are well off, not only your own but other people may also come close to you to benefit from you. But, if you are poor or lack wealth, not only other people but also your own people may turn their back. Not all but only some people are of this nature in our society. There are no medicines for the shamelessness – there are some people in the society who do wrong things shamelessly. There is not any medicine to treat them and change them to be good. However, there are also some courageous people in our society who always work hard despite many obstacles. No moustache can block the mouth to eat indicates those courageous people. And, the proverb where there is a will, there is way tells that those courageous people continue working hard using different methods to overcome obstacles and succeed in the end.'

Grandma cleared her throat and explained the meaning of other sayings. People may have many wishes, but they cannot fulfil all. They can only fulfil those wishes which they can afford relying on their own means. Consider your throat before swallowing a piece of bone – this proverb teaches that people should rely on their capacity to achieve their aim. The throat hole is small but what happens if one tries to swallow a big piece of bone? It chokes in the throat causing death. Therefore, everyone should be aware of their own capacity to fulfil their wishes. There are also some people in society who have things to be done in one place, but they run towards other directions. They are unable to attain their goal even after working hard. The proverb that the work is at one place but going somewhere else gives the lesson to focus on the task what needs to be done at the right place at the right time to attain the set goal.

The proverb whether the real jungle tiger eats you or not, a tiger in your mind may eat you has also a deep meaning and gives important lesson to people. You know that people fear many things. People have fears in their mind such as this may happen or that may happen. There should be fear in mind but with only real problems or dangers which may help them to be aware of those dangers. Sometimes we fear a danger which does not exist but is in our mind. That is not good at all. You should make up your mind based on the reality. There may not be any tiger around, we may think if there is any tiger around which may kill us. People get scared of any strange figure they see suddenly in front of them thinking like a ghost. Likewise, if we see strange people in a lonely place, we may think that they may be thieves and be afraid of them.'

All proverbs are derived from experiences of life and they match with the nature of people one way or another. They provide life lessons. Let me tell you one incident when I was eaten by a tiger in my mind.'

Finally, she came to the story she wanted to tell us. We were listening to her with so much interest.

CHAPTER 41

'It was an incident that happened some twenty years back. I had grown older and was not able to go to our farmland on the next mountain across the river like before. However, I had to go sometimes.' She started the background of the story.

'It was the harvesting season in December. All our farmlands across the river were leased out and we had to go every year during the harvesting season to get paid by the leaseholders. Some used to pay in cash and some in commodity, the farm product itself. That year in December, I had gone there to collect the payments from the leaseholders. I stayed there for three days and collected all the payments. I had already sent home the goods I'd collected with the local porters. Around two thousand Rupees was the cash collected which I had kept securely inside my dress in a locally made cotton purse. I had kept two ten Rupees notes separately making a knot at one corner of my shawl in case I needed it to buy bananas on the way if I could find them. I never used to have much jewellery while travelling alone. However, I had a pair of small earrings and a nasal button of gold.'

When the sun started descending, I set out for home and shortly reached the river. As it was already winter, the river water level was low and could be crossed on foot. However, there was a temporary bridge built for the children and the elderly people. I crossed the river by the bridge. There was a small forest just on the other side of the river from where a steep trail started to climb up the hill to get home.'

Giving a brief location description, she said, 'I was not able to walk fast. I had just started walking up the hill slowly, three unknown men arrived behind me. I got scared. The spot is like a covered corner. In that lonely place, I was an old woman and suspected that they were robbers. They could easily hold me and steal everything I had. In such a mental state, I was very frightened. I let them go ahead of me and sat on the ground on a stone exhaling and pretending as if I was tired even though there was a rest point close a bit up. They proceeded ahead.'

'I thought that they would have gone by then but when I reached the rest point, they were still there sitting on the rest point. I got more scared thinking that they might have been waiting for me. They asked me to take a rest. I did not speak at all and sat on a stone. One of them asked – ma'am, are you coming back collecting your farmland payments? How much money did you make? I became sure that they were planning to steal my money. I spoke softly with fear and told – I have not carried money with me. I have got only this twenty Rupees. Then I showed them the notes taking out from my shawl knot. I extended that twenty rupees to them and said – you can have this.'

'Then they knew that I was afraid of them thinking them robbers. One of them told – Oh! Ma'am you are of thinking that we are robbers. They laughed loud and said again – we know you ma'am, but you did not know us. We are the officers from the district court office. There is a case of the village people across the river in the court and had been there to get a public statement. Hearing them, all my fear vanished completely. Then I also laughed loud together with them. Let's go together, we will walk slowly with you until we cross the forest. The men I was thinking robbers were government officers. I also walked slowly along with them. When we crossed the forest, they went faster leaving me to continue at my own pace.'

'With wrong assumption, I feared the government officers thinking them as robbers. Not a jungle tiger but a tiger in my mind ate me.' She finished the story and laughed loud opening full her toothless mouth. We laughed with her.

CHAPTER 42

While she ended the story about the robbers, grandma thought for a while and told, 'Now, I'll tell you an incident about a cheater. I hope, you are not feeling bored yet, are you?'

'Not at all. We are enjoying it. Please tell us.' I replied.

'My prince.' She said, softly touched my lips with her loving fingers and kissed those fingers herself. It was her a unique style of showing her love to me sometimes.

'Many years back.' She entered this subject matter directly.

'We were sitting in the outer reception room, the porch of our house, in the evening just after the sunset, your grandpa, your dad and me. Your dad was still a baby, may be just five or six years old. Your grandpa was on a bench and I was on the floor. Your dad was with me cuddling. By the door close to the bench, there was a wooden chair.'

'Meanwhile, a man came down to us entering from our compound gate. In the traditional Nepalese dress and Nepalese cap, who might be in his mid-fifties, seemed very clever from his posture and appearance. As you know, we have a tradition to treat anyone who arrives in the evening as god's representative in the form of guest. When the man came in unexpected as a guest in the evening, your grandpa greeted him and requested to take a seat on the chair. I also greeted him and started thinking myself what to offer him for dinner.'

I had an opportunity to reinforce my knowledge about the traditional Nepalese dress and a Nepalese culture to welcome even uninvited guests, too, which I had heard and read before.

'What would you like, tea, squash or fresh juice? Your grandpa asked him. He preferred to have cold water and I went inside to get it for him. I poured water in an *Amkhora* (a bronze jug made locally in the village specially for drinking water, which you might have already seen being made, I hope) from a *Gagro* (a mud pot locally made specially for keeping the drinking water cold). He drank water in a typical village style i.e., he faced upwards, lifted the jug high and poured water opening his mouth in such a way that the jug did not touch his mouth and produced a sound from his throat. He had almost finished the water as he was very thirsty. After drinking the water, he put the jug on the floor and said – how tasty is this drinking water. Yes, people say that the drinking water from our natural spring water source is very tasty – I quickly answered him.' Grandma continued telling.

'Although sun had already set, there was still daylight and it had not turned dark. We could see faces clearly. The guest looked at your grandpa's face carefully for a while and said – awesome, looking at your fate lines on your face, it is noticeably clear that you are an incredibly lucky man. Your grandpa did not like him talking about fate unnecessarily and without being asked for. He never believed about fate lines, birth calendars and astrologers' predictions.'

'Then he replied – you are right mister; I also know that I'm very lucky; as a result of hard work, I'm well off; I've got a loving and caring wife; my children have got their education; grown up sons are progressing well in their professions; small children are studying well; all my married daughters are also well off and doing well; what better fate do I want than this? Nonetheless, such a fate of mine is not due to fate lines on my face but is due to mine and my family's hard work'.

You did not get my point; I meant that your death is to happen in a sacred pilgrim place – the guest said shaking his voice. Your grandpa did not like this prediction of him as well. And, he said – you are again right; I know I will die in a sacred place. If I die in my house, it's a sacred place, if I die by the sacred basil plant right out there in our front yard, it's a sacred place; if I die while I'm at any temple, they are sacred places, too; there is God in every particle of the earth and every place is a sacred place; until we do not do any sin, every place in this world is a sacred pilgrim place; until now I've never thought bad of anybody, I haven't hurt anyone; I'm living my simple life doing my own simple businesses; so, if I die at home or a temple or anywhere, that will be a sacred place for me.

The man did not have good intentions. He might have thought to be welcomed as a guest, have delicious dinner and at the same time get money for his slippery words of fate and luck. He found that he would not be able to cheat your grandpa with his slippery words and stood up from the chair and said, 'I've got to go now.' We requested him to stay overnight as it was almost evening and to go in the morning. But he said that he had to go somewhere else and then left straight away.

'You may see those type of cheaters time and again. Some astrologers may be knowledgeable. But you may see cheaters in the name of astrologers who say that they can read fate lines, birth calendars or pretend being saints. You should not believe them and should not run after their predictions. Did you get it children? Rely on your own capacity and hard work. If you work hard and pray to god with a true heart, your fate is better itself.' Grandma concluded her story.

CHAPTER 43

'Do you want me tell more stories? Not enough for you all?' Seeing us still eager for more stories, she asked us.

'Not enough grandma. Please tell one more for today.' We asked her.

She thought for a while for a story and then began.

'I was just fifteen or sixteen years old.' Grandma was giving us the background of the story. 'I was the only daughter-in-law and never got a break from all the household chores. It was almost evening. I was in the kitchen preparing dinner for the family. My mother-in-law was also in the kitchen sitting in one corner. We were chatting about this and that. It was the rainy season. I could hear the non-stop sound of frogs from outside, croak, croak, croak.

'I used to be very afraid of frogs, especially the toads. When I spotted them, I used to start screaming and jumping high. Are you afraid of frogs as well?' She asked us.

'I'm not.' Rachana replied first. Other friends also said that they were not afraid of frogs. I did not say anything since I'd not seen frogs in the open field that way.

'I needed a broom to clean up the kitchen. When I got to the porch of our house to fetch a broom, suddenly a toad landed right in front of me jumping in from the front yard. What did I need to wait for then? I started screaming and jumping, aah! Hearing my screams, my mother-in-law rushed to me asking what had happened? Seeing the frog and me screaming and jumping, she laughed at me and threw the frog back to the front yard easily with a broom. She said – what will this stupid girl do in her life? Let's go inside; and, we went in together.' Recalling the moment, she was scared by a frog, grandma laughed opening her toothless mouth so wide that I could clearly see the bottom of her tongue. I imagined the scene of the frog and my grandma screaming and jumping. It also took me back to the battles of frogs of *Sabhapokhari* and the demon frog in the story of Frog Stone which she had told us the previous week.

'In the kitchen, my mother-in-law asked me if the meal was ready. I replied that everything else was ready except the rice which just needed to be steamed fully. Then she asked me to leave the rice on a low fire for steaming and to come closer to her. She said that she wanted to tell me a story about a frog and an elephant. When I took a seat close to her, she touched me on my head and started telling the story. I'll tell you the same story now.' Then she told us the story she heard from my great grandma.

CHAPTER 44

Once upon a time, there was a village. There was a forest a bit far away from the village. The villagers used to go to that forest to collect firewood. One day, a father and his son from the village had gone to the forest. The father was in his mid-forties and the son was a teenager, fifteen or sixteen years old. While they were collecting the firewood, they saw an unbelievable scene. There was a frog around fifteen yards away from them. An elephant came close to the frog. When the frog saw the elephant, the size of the frog started growing suddenly and, in the end, the frog became bigger than the elephant. The father and son hid themselves behind a bush and looked at that incredible scene with their eyes wide. In no time, the frog, bigger than the elephant, opened his mouth wide and swallowed the elephant. Seeing such a

horrific scene, both father and son closed their eyes with fear. When they did not hear any sound, they opened their eyes and found that the frog had already disappeared having swallowed the elephant.

I was stunned to hear that a frog became bigger than an elephant and asked, 'Grandma, will you please explain, how could a frog become bigger than an elephant?'

'It's just mythical, my dear. In folklores, you may find such characters who have powers to change their forms and sizes when they want and can do many strange things. Have patience, the story will take you to an end where you will be satisfied. For now, I just tell you that this cannot happen in normal life and therefore, I said earlier it to be an unbelievable scene.' Answering me, she continued her story.

Seeing such a bizarre scene, the man said to his boy – son, we saw such an unbelievable thing. Do not mention it to anyone, even by mistake. The boy agreed with him. Then they returned home quickly carrying the firewood they had collected.

After some time, the boy was with a group of his friends chatting. His friends talked about some funny things. He could not stop himself and mentioned about the incident of a frog swallowing an elephant, which he stated that he had witnessed it personally. His friends did not believe him. He even told that he and his father were together and had seen it but still his friends did not believe him. Then he had a bet with them to prove it by asking his father. All of them went together to his father and asked him if it was true. The boy was shocked when his father said that that was not true. His friends were happy to win the bet and left.

The boy was sad to lose the bet because his father had lied. He had never imagined that his father would lie in that way. He sat on a stone at the corner of their house sulking angrily and with his chin on hands. His father noticed it, but he pretended as if he had got no clue how his son would be feeling and went to their cow shed to give them grass to eat. He thought his father to be a liar. He was extremely disappointed.

When the man finished his job at the cowshed and returned home, his son was still sitting in the same mood. He approached the boy and said – look my dear, don't get upset and angry with me. I had already told you not to mention to anyone about the incident even by mistake, they would not believe it. If I had said yes, they would demand us to prove it. Could we prove it? No, not at all. Then what would happen? They would spread a rumour in the village that both of us, father and son, were mentally sick. They would say that a father gave a false witness. Nobody would believe that we had seen the scene. Because we would not be able to repeat the same scene to prove it.

The man comforted his son on his head and said – Don't get frustrated. I did not lie to make you a loser. Instead, I want to help you win. Do you really want to win bet with your friends, my boy?

Yes, of course I want to win – the boy replied.

Then the man said to him – So, don't worry. I will help you to win for sure. Wait and keep patience for some time. For this, we should do one thing. But, never mention to anyone what we are doing. When I will tell you to go and tell your friends and bet with them, only then you will tell them. Alright?'

The boy became bright and happy when father told him that he would help him to win a bet and he went inside the house with him.

They had a cow due to give birth in couple of days. The cow was kept in a shed opposite of their house. There was a small pond further from the cow shed. The pond was made with the natural spring water and looked clean and fresh always. There was a basil plant container built permanently with bricks and mud at one corner of their front yard.

Let me explain a bit about the importance of the basil plant which will help you understand the story more clearly. The basil plant is regarded as a sacred plant. It is regarded as the soulmate of Lord *Vishnu*. You might have seen a permanent basil plant container in almost every house in their front yards. We have a tradition of performing two rituals with the basil plant, one falls in June and the other in December. The first ritual is the plantation of the basil plant on the day fixed according to Nepalese lunar calendar that falls in June. The ritual follows fasting, sowing basil seeds and worshipping in the end. A nicely built permanent container is filled with manure mixed soil; then the basil seeds are sowed in the container; and, in the end we worship it. We water and worship the basil plant everyday then after.

The second event is carried out again on one fixed day according to the Nepalese lunar calendar that falls in December and this ritual is called *Tulasi Bibah* (Basil Plant Marriage). In this event, a ritual of chanting mantras of marriage procedures by a priest is performed in addition to fasting and worshipping for the marriage of Lord *Vishnu* with the basil plant in that container which I described earlier as his soulmate, an *Avatar* of Goddess *Laxmi*. So, a container with the basil plant is regarded as holy as a temple. Every day, we make three circles of the container clockwise by walking around it and worship the basil plant. This is our religious deed to worship Lord *Vishnu* and Goddess *Laxmi*. Now, I think, you are clear about the importance of basil plant and why that man had a basil plant container in the front yard of his house.

After two days, their cow gave birth to a male calf. The man had taken his son with him at the time the cow gave birth. Immediately after the calf was born, they took him to the pond, cleaned him up, dipped him in the water, brought him to the basil plant container, made three circles of the container clockwise by walking around it with the calf and then took him to have his mother's milk. After that day, during every milking time, morning and evening, they repeated the same process every day. They repeated such a practice for ten days. The boy was always with his father during this practice and he had observed everything.

One morning, the man wanted to test if the calf would do the same thing on his own or not. He released the calf and left it free. The calf went straight to the pond, took a dive, came to the basil plant container and made three circles of it clockwise, then went to his mother and started sucking milk. He tested it in the evening and the following morning, too. Every time the calf repeated it on his own. Now the man was quite sure that the calf had become well practiced and would not miss doing it.

Then the man said to his son – it's the time now for you to win the bet my son. Go and bet with your friend that our calf does not suck his mother's milk without taking a bath in the pond and making three circles of the basil plant container. I know, they won't believe you. Bring them here to prove with evidence by a live show and you will win the bet and be proud without needing anybody to speak in your favour.

The boy went to see his friends with the confidence of winning the bet. They were gathered in one place as usual and chatting. Seeing him there, one of his friends said – do you have any nonsense things to say today? All his friends laughed at him ironically.

He did not get angry from what his friends said. Instead, he was calm and said – listen my friends, there is no guarantee that you guys will win the bet every time. So, don't be so arrogant.

What do you want to bet on today – another boy asked him. He said 'a few days ago, one of our cows gave birth to a calf. But you know, it's so strange, the calf does not suck his mother's milk without taking a bath in the pond and making three circles of the basil plant container.'

'Impossible, it can't happen at all. Can it be believed? How ridiculous it would be that a calf takes bath and walks around a basil plant container before sucking the cow's milk? Today once again, you're talking nonsense, this is a bluff to make us look like fools.' His friends did not believe him. He bet with them and took them to his house.

The sun had already set. It was almost the time for milking the cow. He asked them to wait for a while. Seeing them, his father got ready for milking the cow. He was sure that his son would win the bet. The man went to the cow shed carrying a milking bucket. The boys watched everything standing at a corner of the courtyard.

Reaching the cow shed, the man hung the milking bucket on a hook and freed the calf from the rope it was fastened with. The calf, as practiced, went straight to the pond, dived into the water, went to the basil plant container and made three circles of it walking clockwise, only then he went to his mother and started sucking her milk. The boys were astonished to

see what was happening and stared with eyes wide. This time, the boy won the bet without needing any witness to speak on his favour. His friends were speechless, could not say anything and returned their homes losing the bet.

Grandma finished the story and told as usual the closing verse – 'to the listeners, gold's garland. . .' and asked us, 'What lesson does this story give us, children?'

We could not instantly answer to her question. Seeing that we were confused, she explained the lesson herself, 'If you can't prove anything even it is the truth, do not mention it to anyone. It happens to be like the story of a frog swallowing an elephant. Nobody will believe it and we will be proved liars in society. Like a saying – even the God of Truth is considered a liar if he alone is without evidence. The story of the calf gives a lesson that a continuous practice may make things possible that may seem impossible in an ordinary situation. Therefore, hard work and a continuous practice is the key to your success. Likewise, you should study hard and should have continuous practice to be successful in your life.'

Thanks grandma, she gave such an important lesson at the end of the story. I felt that my grandma was not only a good storyteller, but she was also an experienced teacher. At the end, she said, 'that's it for today. I'll tell other stories next time' and as usual, after speaking, she pushed her lips into her toothless mouth, pretended as if chewing them and produced her usual sound from the throat, kraunk, kraunk, kraunk.

CHAPTER 45

It had been a month since I came to the village. My return date had already come, it was just the following day. And, it was my last day in the village. We would be taking a bus the next day afternoon to the airport, stay overnight there and fly to Kathmandu the following morning. Yes, it was my last Saturday in the village and we had planned to visit *Waleshwor* cave that day.

As on the previous Saturdays, we set out for *Waleshwor* cave after our breakfast. My friends told me that we needed torches for the light inside the cave and worshipping stuff to worship *Shivlinga* (Lord *Shiva's* figurine) which was in the cave. However, they told me not to worry because they had already arranged and carried the things with them.

My friends had shown me from our courtyard a small village at the bottom of the hill and said that the village was called *Wala*. They also said that there is a cave below that village on a difficult steep rocky slope. Since it is in *Wala* village, it is called *Waleshwor*. After half an hour, we reached a trekkers' rest point some three hundred meters from the cave, from where a rocky cliff begins, and a narrow trail goes through it to go to the cave. This was the only path to reach the cave.

We started walking slowly towards the cave through the narrow trail. While walking through that dangerous narrow path, I felt dizzy for a moment when I looked downwards and my entire body puffed-up. I stopped, closed my eyes, strengthened myself and then again walked ahead slowly. I was at the middle of the line; three friends were ahead of me and three behind. They were, of course, well used to walking through it and could probably even run on this path. But I had to take support of the wall from time to time. The path was so narrow that two people from opposite directions had to carefully give way to pass each other. If by some reason someone would fall down the cliff, there was no chance that they would survive and would have no chance even to say ouch!

'Are you scared Robin? Do you need support? Extend your hand.' By the time Sweta, who was just ahead of me, said this, I was getting the hang of it.

'No, thanks.' I replied. However, walking through that narrow trail in such a steep difficult place was really an adventure for me and I kept on walking along with my friends being careful.

People had made a flat space by cutting the hard rock at the entrance of the cave. Perhaps, it was a place for visitors to wait. There was a three-tiered platform made from stones at one corner and at the other corner, there were two wooden benches. Right at the entrance, at one side, there was a grey-coloured rounded stone of about three meters in diameter which looked like a mound.

We sat on the benches for a while and took stuff out from our bags to carry inside the cave. Sachin, Nirav and Eashan took a torch each. Sweta, Rachana and Sirjana carried stuff for worshipping the *Shivalinga*. They did not give me anything of those stuff to carry. Nevertheless, I had carried my camera and pen and notebook in my small bag.

We went into the cave and moved slowly and carefully. Among the friends holding torches, one was at the front, one at the middle and the other one behind us.

Light from the three torches was enough for us. While we were moving forward inside the cave, Nirav told me, 'You know Robin, the *Shivlinga* in this cave is the largest in the world. It is two metres in diameter and it's about the same size as a one and half metres tall.' I thanked Nirav for the new information. Not only Nirav, but all of those my friends were good sources of knowledge for me. I had learnt many things from them. I felt lucky to have such knowledgeable friends.

It took around five minutes to reach our destination inside the cave. There was a spacious spot at the end of the cave. What I saw in that space made my eyes go even wider with amazement.

Unbelievable! The word came out of my mouth without me knowing and my friends looked at me. There was a big stone which exactly looked like a *Shivlinga* on the ground. Just above the *Shivlinga* in the rock, there was an object hanging but inbuilt in the rock that looked exactly like a cow's udder with four teats. More surprisingly, milk like white fluid from all four teats was dripping down directly on the *Shivlinga*. Friends told me – people believe that nobody made them, but they were natural and the *Shivlinga* has been irrigated non-stop like that since long ago. There was no reason that I would not take photographs of that astonishing scene. Since it was in the cave, there was no light like outside. So, I got my friends to flash the torches nicely and with the help of my camera's flash, I took several photos.

'Are there any stories about this cave, too?' I expressed my curiosity.

'There should be for sure. We will ask grandma when we return home.' Nirav said.

All of us took our share of the worshipping stuff that included flowers and wood apple plant's leaves, red and yellow powders, wet and red coloured rice, fruits and red and white cloth pieces and offered them to the *Shivlinga* (named as *Waleshwor*). Sweta had carried cow milk in a small bottle which we poured little by little and turn by turn on *Shivlinga* as a tradition of irrigating it and as a part of worshipping *Shivlinga*. After finishing worshipping, we came out of the cave. We sat on the bench, while I took notes of important points about the cave and the *Shivlinga*. We had to return home a bit early that day. We walked back through the same narrow path but this time I was used to it and could walk with my friends normally. Walking past the narrow trail, we rested for about ten minutes at the rest point and started walking up towards our house. Just before three o'clock in the afternoon, we reached home, and we all had our afternoon snacks together.

Because my return date had come, I could see sad faces of all the family. Most of all, grandma looked very much sad. She had poured her love on me and my sister almost every day giving a hug firmly and kissing our foreheads.

'How did you find your family village, Robin?' It was my aunt who asked while we were having our afternoon snacks.

'I found it so beautiful aunty that I can't express it in words. I don't want to go back. But, what can I do? We live in London and I must go. On top of that, my school is there and will open from next week. So, I've got to go back, unwillingly.' I said.

CHAPTER 46

After we finished our snacks, we went in front of grandma and took our seats as usual. I asked her to tell the story, first, about the *Waleshwor* cave.

She started, 'The story of *Waleshwor* is related to Lord *Shiva*, which is clear from the *Shivlinga* which you saw in the cave. Isn't that right, my dear?'

I nodded agreeing with her.

'Long ago, in the prehistoric era called *Satyayug*,' she started the story, 'A demon performed an extremely hard and rigorous meditation praying to Lord *Shiva*. It is believed that Lord *Shiva* would bless the devotee what they wished if he is pleased with the prayer, and it is also a God's rule, it is believed. Lord *Shiva* was pleased with the demon's meditation and prayer. He appeared in front of him and asked what his wish was. The demon did not lose the opportunity and asked to bless him with such a spiritual power that he could be able to turn anyone to ash instantly by placing his hand on the head of. Lord *Shiva*, without thinking anything, blessed him with the power.'

'When that evil creature was blessed, he told Lord *Shiva* that he would go from there only after he tested the blessing and he wanted to put his hand on Lord *Shiva*'s head himself for a test. Lord *Shiva* knew his trick would finish him off and ran away from him. The demon started chasing him. In this escape effort, Lord *Shiva* made narrow caves on the  Rocky Mountains to hide himself, where the giant demon was not able to get in. Hiding for a while, Lord *Shiva* came out of the cave thinking that the demon would have gone away but he found him waiting. Seeing him waiting, Lord *Shiva* ran away again to another mountain, made another narrow cave and hid himself inside. In this way, he made many caves on different mountains. In the end, Lord *Shiva* made the

Waleshwor cave, where you have already been today, and he was hiding inside and the demon waiting for him outside. From the god's kingdom, other gods were observing the hide and seek game.'

'Lord *Vishnu*, the cleverest god among all gods, thought that the demon would not spare Lord *Shiva* and, hence, had to do something. The demons, by their nature, used to be infatuated easily with pretty lasses. Lord *Vishnu* was aware of their nature and he took the form of a very beautiful young woman and went close to him. The demon, as expected, was besotted to see a pretty girl just in front of him that he could not move his eyes away from her. Taking advantage of the situation, the girl started further mesmerising him with her sweet and tuneful words. She asked him why a brave and great personality like him, who could control over all three worlds of heaven, earth and netherworld, was sitting in that lonely rough mountain. Being mesmerised by her, he told everything about the blessing he received and waiting for Lord *Shiva* to test the blessing on his head. Criticizing Lord *Shiva*, the girl told him that Lord *Shiva* is a powerful god just for namesake and not to believe in his blessings. She said that his blessing would not have any effect and would never come true. She further influenced him by her mesmerising voice of an angel why he was running after him for such a minor test and advised him to test placing his hand on his own head to prove his blessing false.'

'The demon was fully influenced by her sweet words, did not think of anything else, put his hand on his head and turned to ash there and then. Lord *Vishnu* returned to his real form and went back to the gods' kingdom taking Lord *Shiva* with him. Because the demon was turned into ash, he got his name then after to be *Bhasmasur,* meaning an Ash Demon. The stone looking like a hump at the entrance of the cave is the pile of his ash which turned into stone over time. The spot inside the cave where Lord *Shiva* was hiding, a *Shivlinga* was generated naturally immediately after he left the cave. In honour of Lord *Shiva*, the mother earth created a cow's udder and teats right above the *Shivalinga* and started irrigating it by dripping milk like fluid on it since then, which has continued till today. To the listeners – gold's garland . . .' Grandma finished the story about the *Waleshwor* cave.

'Did you like the story about *Waleshwor,* Robin?' Grandma asked.

'It was interesting, grandma. I liked it very much. Please tell us the next story.' I replied and asked her for another story.

CHAPTER 47

Grandma got ready to tell another story. She cleared her throat. Then, as it was her habit, she pushed her lips into her toothless mouth, pretended of chewing and produced her peculiar sound of kraunk, kraunk, kraunk. We were just waiting for her.

'Now, I will tell you about an incident that happened at a sea beach far away from our village, ok children?'

We replied together, 'That would be great as well.'

You should still remember the story about a golden snake that had wrapped me. I've also told you what I saw and what they told me when the snake goddess took me to their palace in the snake kingdom. I'd seen them all having a maroon-coloured line painted upright on their forehead above their serpent jewels and them singing Lord *Vishnu's* verses. The king snake had told me, 'You would be a Lord *Vishnu* devotee like us; our devotion path is the same; therefore, we brought you here to bless you; we do not bring everyone but only selected.' The story begins right from there.

After that incident, I felt that my inclination towards Lord *Vishnu* increased unknowingly. I became very much interested in following the path to Lord *Vishu* having similar maroon coloured line painted on my forehead. But, what could I do? I never got free time from the household chores to go for it. For many years, my interest was suppressed in my mind.

When my children grew up, sons got married and daughters-in-law came in, then I got time to travel around. Your grandpa started taking me for pilgrimages. I have visited *Pashupatinath*, *Muktinath*, *Vishwanath*, *Badri Kedar*, *Brindaban* and many other pilgrim destinations together with your grandpa. But with the god's will, your grandpa passed away. I felt very lonely. Who would take me for the pilgrimages? My sons and daughters-in-law were busy in their jobs and household matters. So, unknowingly, I started looking for a friend circle. In the end, I met a group of Lord *Vishnu's* devotees in the *Terai* (the plain region) through my eldest daughter and I was also converted as a devotee of Lord *Vishnu* from my traditional path.

Do you see the line painted on my forehead? I must paint this line fresh every morning. She showed her maroon coloured line painted on her forehead and continued telling the story.

It came true what the snake gods and goddesses had told me. I followed the same devotion path as them; I have same maroon coloured line painted on my forehead and enjoyed singing Lord *Vishnu's* verses, *Shreeman Narayan*. After that, I have gone for pilgrimage many times along with the devotees' group. The most sacred pilgrim destination for us is the temple of *Venkatesh* in south India. I have visited the temple almost every year since I started to follow the devotion path. We used to visit a temple called *Rameshwaram* as well when we visited the *Venketesh* temple. But, for the past eight or ten years, I have not been able to go for pilgrimage due to my old age.

The temple of *Rameshwaram* is at the southern end of India at seashore. The temple of *Rameshwaram* is related to the story of Lord *Ram* in the prehistoric era called *Tretayug* when Lord *Ram's* wife *Sita* was abducted and taken to *Lanka* (present day's Sri Lanka) by *Rawan*, the then king of *Lanka*. The stories are about the victory of Lord *Ram* over *Rawan*; how *Hanuman*, a giant monkey, jumped across the sea and reached *Lanka* to find *Sita*; a snake goddess called *Surasa* took a form of a giant sea demon much bigger than *Hanuman* in size to test his power; she tried to swallow *Hanuman* but he came out from her ear entering from her mouth; *Hanuman* burnt the city of *Lanka*; the monkey force of Lord *Ram* built a bridge called *Setu* across the sea to reach *Lanka*; and, many more such interesting stories. However, I am not going into those stories now. Instead, I want to tell you about an incident that happened at *Rameshwaram* when I was there for pilgrimage.

One morning, I had gone to take a bath in the sea together with my friends before going into the temple. My friends were a bit further away from me. At the spot where I was, there was a teenage boy of fifteen- or sixteen-years old standing by the water. A bit further away from him, some ten yards away, there was a man, who looked in his sixties, observing the boy. I was close to the boy and I also observed his activities with interest. There was a village at that seaside, may be a mile away from the spot. The boy and the man were both from that village and they knew each other, which I learnt from them later.

The boy was doing an interesting thing. When there were waves coming from the sea, they used to reach the sand and upon returning, some fish brought by the waves were left on the sand and the fish started jumping. The boy was picking up those fish and throwing them back to the water every time the waves came.

After observing the boy for a while, the man came close to him and said, 'I see you here at this time every day and throwing fish back to the water. Why are you doing this, dear?'

'The fish left on the sand by the waves will die. If I throw them back to the water, they will survive. I am doing this to save them. I've given one hour of my time every day to do this and I'm trying to save as many fish as I can.' The boy replied simply.

'I appreciate your thought, dear. But there are so many seas and oceans on the earth. Hundreds of thousands of waves come and go every moment, they leave millions of fish on the sand and they are dying. What will it make difference to the planet if you throw only a few fish back to the water?' The man asked again.

The boy replied calmly, 'I don't know what it will make difference to the planet. But I know that it will definitely make difference to the life of the fish I throw back to the water and that is what I want.'

The man became speechless hearing the reply of the boy and went quietly from there. I was also surprised to hear the boy. From his work and what he said, I learnt a big lesson. I learnt that helping poor, helpless and troubled people is the real devotion to the god. If we can bring their smile back, god will also be happy. Since then, following the lesson from that boy, I have been helping the needy people in whatever way I can. I wish you children to be interested in helping the needy people from your own place.

Brilliant! The story was not only interesting but also giving a far-reaching lesson. I thanked grandma a lot for such an invaluable story. My respect for her increased a lot.

'How did you find the story, my dear?' She asked me.

'I liked it very much. Thank you, grandma'. I replied.

Then she called me close to her, comforted me on my cheeks, said 'my prince, my good boy' and kissed me on my forehead, muah, muah, muah.

CHAPTER 48

After telling the story about a boy and fish, grandma cleared her throat and started background of another story.

'Many years back.' Grandma said, 'Your grandpa had taken me for pilgrimage to the *Pashupatinath* temple in Kathmandu during a special festival called *Mahashivratri.*'

There were no vehicles and road transportation those days like we have today in our village. After walking up and down the mountains for three days, we reached a city called *Dharan*. There was no direct bus from *Dharan* to *Kathmandu*, too. We had to take a bus one day to one of the two cities called *Janakpur* and *Birganj* and the following day, another bus to *Kathmandu*. Your grandpa planned to go to *Janakpur* and spend one day to visit a famous temple called *Janaki* temple.

The city of *Janakpur* is famous for two reasons. First, the *Janaki* temple itself and second, the traditional fine art of the region called *Mithila* Art. I got a good opportunity to visit the temple but there was not any exhibition or museum of the *Mithila* Art in the city that I could visit. Therefore, I did not get any opportunity to see the *Mithila* Art satisfactorily except those painted on the walls of some houses by the house owners themselves. My interest is still unfulfilled. That is a typical and indigenous tradition of the region. They are beautiful. That must be preserved and promoted. If not an Art Museum, the *Mithila Art* could be used to paint the whole story of the *Ramayan* around the *Janaki Temple.* This would not only attract more visitors but would also extend the stay of the visitors in the city, thus, contributing more towards the local economy. Why don't the local people have such a simple vision, too?'

Including one day's stay in the city of *Janakpur*, we reached our destination, Kathmandu, six days after we left home. It was crowded everywhere; thousands of people had come to observe the *Mahashivaratri* festival. There were no rooms available for us to stay in the public rest houses. Thank god, one of your grandpa's friends had his house nearby. The temple of *Pashupatinath* and the streets around it were too crowded on the festival day. Where had that many people come from? I saw folks in different dresses from across the country, east, west, hills and the *Terai*, from everywhere. People had come from India, too. Not only ordinary people, there was a remarkable gathering of all types of saints, from enlightened saints to ordinary hermits.

As I said, there were a few enlightened saints. One of them was *Shyamchetan Baba*, an enlightened saint, who had already crossed hundred years of age, used to live in a house in the temple complex. People had a belief that whoever he would put his hand on their heads and bless them, his blessings would come true. Your grandpa took me first to see him to get his blessings. People were waiting for their turn in a queue, and we lined up. After half an hour, it was our turn. Although the saint was over a hundred years old, he had a different shine in his face. He flashed a warm smile and seemed as if he had spiritual powers. He put his right hand on our heads one after another and blessed us with happiness, prosperity and good health.

After we were blessed by *Shyamchetan Baba*, we came out of his room, went to worship Lord *Pashupatinath* and stood in an exceptionally long queue of the worshippers. It took almost three and half hours to reach the main door of the temple. Finishing the main task of worshipping in the temple, we made three rounds of the temple, clockwise. There were several sacred fireplaces burning big wooden logs around the temple and there was crowd of people taking warmth from the holy fire. We walked down to the river at the back of the temple through nicely paved stone steps. In the river, there were people taking their bath to get ready for worshipping in the temple. We had already taken our bath in the morning. There were a few sacred fireplaces at the bank of the river, too. A crowd of people including hermits were around those fireplaces, too, to take warmth of the holy fire.

Meanwhile, I heard someone saying that there was an enlightened saint in meditation in the forest called *Shleshmantak* on the hilltop across the river and he could tell the past, present and future of anyone very correctly with his meditation power. I became eager to see him and ask him about past, present and future of my family. I asked your grandpa to take me to see him. He refused initially but I insisted. We crossed the river over a bridge and climbed up to the hilltop through stone steps. After a while, we were in front of the saint who was in meditation and he had his eyes closed. There were other people waiting for him, too.

People said that the saint had been coming every year one month in advance of the festival and would sit for meditation at the same spot. People had heard about him and many people used to come every day to know their past, present and future from him.

Two teenage boys also heard about him and they planned to test him. They came over to the spot. On the way, they had caught a butterfly and one of the boys was carrying it in his cupped hands. They had planned to ask the saint if the butterfly was dead or alive. If he said alive, they would crush it with their hands and kill but if he said it was dead, then they would release it to fly away. The time those boys arrived, the saint was still in meditation and he had not opened his eyes.

When the boys saw him in meditation, they disturbed him and said, 'Open your eyes Mr. Saint, we have to ask one thing with you.' When the boys called him, he opened his eyes. Seeing them, the saint smiled pleasantly. Perhaps, he knew their intention, he calmly told them, 'Ask, what you have to dear boys.'

'The boy who was carrying the butterfly in his cupped hands asked, 'We heard, you can tell about past, present and future. If so, tell us if the butterfly in my hands is dead or alive.'

'The saint knew their hidden intention and said, 'Dear, whether that butterfly is to be dead or alive is in your hands. If you crush it, it will die; if you release it, it will be alive.'

'Because the saint knew their intention, the faces of the boys turned red with regret, they released the butterfly to fly away and they left. After they had gone, the saint said, 'It was just their funny way of thinking, but they had no intention of harming the butterfly.'

Grandma concluded her story and said, 'You know children, people may have both positive and negative thinking. Always think positively. What lesson does this story give? Ok, leave it to me, I'll tell you myself. You study, prepare your lessons and gain knowledge. You might have also learnt many lessons from the stories I told you. Whether you want all your learnings to be kept alive or let them die is totally in your hands. You must always try to keep them alive. Never forget this to make progress in your life.'

At the end of the story, grandma explained the lesson from it, too. How my friends perceived the lesson, I don't know but for me, it was invaluable. My grandma! I again thanked her.

CHPATER 49

Complete silence! You could hear a pin drop in the room. Grandma had paused after she told the story of the Saint. We were looking at her with our mouths shut.

She broke the silence and asked, 'Is that enough for now?'

'Please tell us another interesting story that has a lesson, grandma.' I asked her.

How could my grandma refuse her lovely grandson's request? She was instantly ready. She thought for a while selecting a story and said, 'But, this story is a bit short. Is that Ok?'

'That's fine.' I replied and grandma started the story.

Once upon a time, there was a family in a village. In the family, there were an old couple and their three sons had already come to marriage age. They decided to get them married and arranged girls for them. Finally, they got them all married one after another and brought three daughters-in-law within a month. They found all three girls well mannered. However, since the girls had come from three different families, they planned to test the wisdom of the girls.

They planned to give responsibilities of the household to all three couples of their sons and daughters-in-law independently and go for a pilgrimage for five years. They called them and mentioned their intent. Their sons and daughters-in-law agreed to this.

When they agreed, the father said, 'Look my dears, there may arise misunderstanding if all you three couples live together in our absence. So, we have decided to assign you separate lands and houses for the time being so that you can handle responsibilities independently until we come back. What do you say to that?'

All three couples agreed and said, 'If you want it that way, we will agree to that.'

They had three houses. The father assigned a separate house and a piece of land for each couple. Before they left for the pilgrimage, they helped them settle well in their respective houses. At the end, the father went to see each couple separately, one after another, carrying with him a package of one kilogram of wheat grain for each but without their knowledge. He tactfully sent his sons out from the house, while visiting every couple; gave the package of wheat to each of his daughters-in-law and said, 'Dear, this is very fine wheat grain. I want you to keep it for me secretly while I am on pilgrimage. Take care of it. You should return it when I come back.' The couple then went on their pilgrimage.

None of the girls knew that the other two were also given the similar packages, which they kept secret. The eldest daughter-in-law kept it in the storeroom secretly. The middle one thought that it might be misplaced in five years' time and, therefore, she kept it in her box locked. The youngest one thought differently. She sowed it in their piece of land instead of keeping in the house. One-kilogram wheat seed yielded almost five kilograms when harvested. She did not use it for themselves, instead she sowed all five kilograms next year again. From the second years' cropping, she had a yield of about twenty kilograms of wheat. She sold the wheat keeping five kilos as seed for another cropping season and saved the cash. She repeated this every year. However, she did not sell the harvest of fifth year but stored it for her in-laws. In this way, after five years, she made a good sum of money as well as fresh wheat full of a storage tank to return to his father-in-law.

The old couple came back home after five years as planned. The old man first went to see his eldest daughter-in-law and asked her to return the wheat. She went to the storeroom to fetch the wheat. Unfortunately, the wheat had already been eaten up by mice and found only a small piece of cloth in which the wheat was packed and one or two pieces of eaten wheat grains. She came with that piece of cloth, told him with shame that the mice had eaten up and begged for a pardon.

He said, 'Don't worry dear. What could you do with the mice? So, forget it.' Then he went to see the middle daughter-in-law. He asked her to return his wheat, too. She went to her room, took out the package of wheat grain from the box and gave it to him. When he opened the package, he found that the wheat was already decomposed and totally turned into the dust. Finding this he said, 'This is rotten and turned into dust. What to do with this? Bin it. But, don't worry, it was beyond your control.' The girl begged for a pardon for not being able to take care of it nicely.

In the end, he went to see the youngest daughter-in-law. He asked her, like other two, to return the wheat he had given to her. First, she was hesitated a while to tell the truth thinking he might be upset why she had sowed the wheat which was given to keep safe. However, she encouraged herself and told the truth, 'Papa, I thought the wheat you gave me would be rotten or misplaced and, therefore, I sowed it in our piece of land. From that one-kilogram wheat you gave me, I got five kilograms yield in the first year. Then in the second year, I sowed all five kilograms and I got twenty kilograms yield. I sold it keeping aside five kilograms for seed and I did it every year.'

'I have not sold the wheat of fifth year, which I have stored for you in the storage tank. You can now have it. I have saved all the money I got from the sale of wheat which came to this much and please take it.' She extended her hand with money and gave it to him. The old man was happy hearing his youngest daughter-in-law. He found her wise, practical and an entrepreneur. He felt proud of her. He returned the money to her and said, 'Keep it yourself. I don't need it. I wanted to test your wisdom and I found in you what I wanted to see. If it is with you, it is for us, too. Now, we live with you. I am sure that you can take care of us during our old age with such your wisdom and creativity.'

The girl was happy that her father-in-law valued and commended her thought and endeavour. Afterwards, the old couple distributed their properties among three sons and themselves and started living happily with the youngest son and daughter-in-law.

Dear children, this story also gives an important lesson. It gives insights that whatever we have good things are as seeds, we should not let them vanish instead we should spread them and grow them creatively. The seed you have is nothing but the knowledge you gain from your education. Not only try to save it but also try to spread it. This is my advice to you as well as my blessing. The story is over now. To the listeners – gold's garland; to the teller – flower's garland; may this story go direct to the god's land.'

CHAPTER 50

Since, it was the last time for me in my trip to hear stories from my grandma, I wanted to hear more and more from her.

'Please tell me one more story, grandma.' I asked as I noticed that she was about to end the session with the story of three daughters-in-law.

'Do you still want more? Which story should I tell now?' I clearly read on her face that she had still energy to tell stories.

'Please tell the story about *Banjhankri*. Robin will like it.' Sweta suggested.

'Ok, ok, about *Banjhankri*. But, let me talk about some matters within the family first.' She looked at us for our agreement.

We nodded.

Then, she cleared her throat and as her habit, she produced a peculiar sound from the bottom of her tongue after pretending chewing her lips. She cleared her throat once more.

Some thirty to thirty-five years back, my youngest daughter, your aunt, fell seriously ill. She has her family in the *Terai,* and she was ill there. It was a very strange and uncommon illness. She could not bend her backbone at all. Because of the illness, she could neither sit down nor do any work. She could walk straight or could lay down straight but could not bend. What a problem! She visited all the hospitals and saw all relevant doctors locally, but no cure. Then she was taken to a well-equipped hospital in *Darbhanga*, India and admitted in the hospital. Many doctors carried out many check-ups in the hospital; blood, stool, urine, x-ray, scan everything and was given a number of medicines. She had her whole body plastered and was laid out on the bed for six months. But there was no progress at all. In the end, the doctors decided that her illness was incurable, they discharged her from the hospital, removed her plaster and sent back home. In such a condition, she wanted to come to us, her parental home and we brought her here carried by porters.

Being her mother, I could always not see her laying down like a wooden log. I thought about getting her treated by a well knowledgeable faith healer. Your grandpa was saying to treat with the herbal plants as well. He was quite knowledgeable on traditional herbal medicines. On top of that he had not much belief on the faith healers. Whereas I had a small hope if I could consult a good shaman.

It was in my mind that there was a *Bizuwa* (a shaman, faith healer, in local language), an old man, in a village down at the bottom of the hill called *Chapabhuin*. He was exceptionally a good shaman, and his treatment had been found to be very effective. People say that he was taken away by *Banjhankris* (wild shamans) and taught shamanism for five years. I had also heard that he had cured many illnesses which were thought to be incurable by the doctors. Hence, I decided to get my daughter treated by him.

'What is a *Banjhankri*, grandma?' I asked.

'Stay patient, my dear. I will explain it for you, later.'
She replied.

One day early in the morning, I sent a man from our village to call and bring the *Bizuwa* (shaman). He was an old man and he had come by walking with a support stick. They arrived at our home around one o'clock in the afternoon. Immediately after he arrived, he started checking my daughter. He caught her wrist with his thumb, forefinger and middle finger and hummed his *mantras* in a peculiar language for a few moments closing his eyes. He was trying to find out what the illness was and what condition. When he finished the check up, he let go off her and opened his eyes. Then he told us – she has been caught by a powerful evil spirit of the *Terai*. He has already caught her very strongly. You brought her to me late. If you had brought her on time at the early stage, I would have cured her easily. Now, I feel that it will be awfully hard for me to send the evil spirit out from her body. But, don't worry, I'll try my best. It may take two to three months. If there will be an effect of my treatment, an abscess will appear in her body. The abscess will grow gradually and at the end, it will burst itself. The illness will come out of her body through the burst abscess in the form of pus and she will get well. After I start treatment, if you see any abscess in her body, let me  know and understand that my treatment has been effective. For my treatment, I will need a black male chick and pure flour of maize. Please arrange them, ma'am.

I gave five Rupees note to the man whom I had sent to call the *Bizuwa* and asked him to find and buy a black male chick going even to every door in the village. I got maize ready and went to get it ground for the flour. It took almost an hour to arrange the required things. After the black chick and the maize flour were ready, the *Bizuwa* started his treatment process. The chick was kept close to him covered by a bamboo net basket. He picked up one spoonful of maize flour with his thumb, forefinger and middle finger, closed his eyes and pronounced his *mantras* (verses) very softly for a while. When he completed his *mantras*, he touched the patient's body moving from her head to leg with his fingers having maize flour and threw the flour to the chick. He repeated this process three times. He had brought some leaves of a plant with him on the way while coming to us which he used as medicine. When he finished the maize flour treatment, he took three leaves out from his bag, crushed them with his palms and fed one drop into the patient's mouth.

He had finished for the day. He stood up from his seat and said, 'All is done for today, ma'am. Keep this chick safe covering it always like this by the bamboo net basket. Never release it. Give it its feed inside the basket. I shall leave now. I'll come back once a week on the market day and carry out my treatment weekly.

I thanked him, gave him fifty Rupees and asked, 'Do you need somebody to accompany you to go home?'

Getting fifty Rupees, he was happy. He said, 'No, thanks. I will go on my own. My own village, it is just a bit away. I always come and go alone,' and left. Then he came back regularly every week on market day and carried out his treatment.

Surprisingly! After five weeks, as he had said, a small abscess appeared on her lower stomach on the right side. When we saw it, we were extremely happy. A hope had emerged that my daughter would get well. When the man came that week for his treatment and saw the abscess, he had a smile of victory on his lips and said, 'My treatment has shown effect.' The patient did not feel any pain and discomfort with the abscess, which gradually grew bigger and looked red and full of pus.

Nine weeks elapsed since he started his treatment. The chick had also grown into a black cockerel and had already started crowing. In the tenth week, the *Bizuwa* had come for his regular treatment process. That day, when the man carried out his process and threw the maize flour to the cockerel inside the bamboo basket third time, the cockerel died there and then. At the same time, the abscess of the patient burst itself and the pus started flowing out massively. Oh my god, so much pus, almost one litre. The hole in the wound was so big it seemed we could put our whole fist into it.

Raising his head high proud on his success, the old man said, 'This poor girl was caught very strongly by the evil spirit. I had to struggle extremely hard to please him. However, I have been able to please him by offering the black cockerel. Now your daughter will get well completely. It may take some time to heal the wound. Ma'am clean up the wound with clean water and dry it up with a clean piece of cloth. I will apply an ointment made from some medicinal plants. Then we will ask her to bend.'

Having said this, he went to the courtyard with a jug of water, cleaned up a piece of flat stone and crushed some leaves he had brought with him with the help of another round shaped piece of stone to make the ointment. In the meantime, I also cleaned up her wound and dried it up with a clean piece of cloth. He applied the ointment on the wound with his light hand. He gave the remaining ointment to me and said to apply it once a day until the wound is completely healed. He buried the dead cockerel in the earth while performing a ritual of chanting his *mantras*.

Miracle! What a great surprise! After applying the ointment, when we asked her to stand up from the bed and bend her body, she could bend it easily without any pain or discomfort. She only felt pain in the wound. She had a big wound and obviously would feel some pain. When the wound had healed in two weeks' time, my daughter was completely fine and since then, she has never had any problem in bending to this day.

That day, I asked the *Bizuwa* where he got such a powerful knowledge from. He told that he got the knowledge from *Banjhankris* and told a story of how he got it. I will tell you the same story he told us, ok? It is interesting. Before the story, let me tell you about *Banjhankris*. Who are they? Where do they live?

CHAPTER 51

Banjhankri!

Ban in local language means forest or wild and *Jhankri* means shaman. From the combination of these two words of local language, they get their name to be *Banjhankri*.

People have different beliefs about *Banjhankris*. However, the common belief is that they are wild humans. They live in caves in the forests. They look like humans. The next common belief among the people about them is that they are shamans. They have spiritual powers to access to the world of evil spirits and to influence them, especially during healing of the illnesses.

Some people believe that they are bigger than a normal human being. They have long golden hair touching the ground. Female *Banjhankris* have big and long breasts that hang below their knees. Therefore, while walking, they keep their breasts up on their shoulders. The female *Banjhankris* will kill humans and eat their fresh flesh. The male *Banjhankris* protect the humans whom they have taken with them from the females. When they meet any human, only males, on the way during they are out from the cave in search of their food, they take him with them, teach them faith healing methods and *mantras* (shamanism) for few days and bring them back safely to the same spot from where they were picked up.

Others believe that *Banjhankris* are half the size of humans. They have long golden hair touching the ground. As they have golden hair some call them *Sunjhankri*, too, deriving the word *Sun* in local language meaning gold and *Jhankri* meaning shaman as in *Banjhankri*. Some others also believe that they are of two types, *Banjhankris* and *Sunjhankris*. Although they are smaller in size than humans, they are extraordinarily strong and powerful. They do not harm humans. Not even the females harm humans as believed by some others. Instead they want to help human beings. They have their own world. In order to help the humans, they come into the human world time to time from their world. They come to and roam around the human world to protect humans from different types of evil spirits who are walking invisible and harm humans.

Banjhankris are angels. They possess spiritual powers. Because they have spiritual powers, people believe, if anybody gets into a river carrying a piece of *Banjhankri's* bone, the river starts flowing in the opposite direction; if you stand in front of a mirror carrying a *Banjhankri's* bone, there will be no your image in the mirror. So, *Banjhankri's* bone is believed to be highly valuable and I have heard that there are stories of people searching high and low for it.

They walk so fast, like a flash. So, ordinary people cannot see them. Whoever they take with them to give the knowledge of shamanism, only those people have seen them. But they do not take everyone, neither they select randomly. They take with them only those people whom they come across the shadow of, even walking in a flash speed. They believe that they will have an adverse effect on their world if they come across the shadow of humans, but only male humans. The only remedy of such adverse effect is to teach them shamanism and make them capable faith healers. Therefore, out of millions, only a few people are taken by *Banjhankris*. They keep the faith healers with them for five years and upon completion of the course, they bring them back and leave at the same spot from where they were picked up. But, strangely, our five years are just five days in the *Banjhankris'* world. Therefore, some people taken by *Banjhankris* say that they had been for five days and some other say five years.

CHAPTER 52

It was interesting to learn something about *Banjhankris.*

'Now, I'll tell you about the story of the *Bizuwa* (our faith healer) what he had told us.' Grandma continued her story.

'Perhaps, the shadow of the *Bizuwa,* our faith healer, also fell on *Banjhankris.* According to him, when he was returned by the *Banjhankris* after completion of his course, five years had already elapsed. Now, listen to his story he told us, which is so interesting.'

His story goes sixty years back. He was just a young boy, ten or eleven-year-old. Those days, there were no schools in their village, nor in the surrounding villages and therefore, the village children were not sent to school. They used to help their parents with their work. He used to work as a goat herder and everyday he used to take his goats for grazing to a lush cliff. One day, he had left his goats grazing and at one point, he was looking down from the top of the cliff to find where his goats were, he felt like a flash hit him and in a moment, he found himself in a completely different and strange world. Let me describe further in his own words.

There were humans like creatures but smaller than me in size. Although the *Banjhankris* were smaller, they were prettier than human beings. The *Banjhakri* girls were so pretty that if there were such pretty girls in the human world, the boys would die for them. Despite such a beautiful face and body construct, they had three strange things. First, their hair was golden and reached the ground. Second, their ears were bigger than of humans and upright and pointed like a rabbit's ears. Third, their feet were unusually big and thick and pointed backwards. However, despite these three unusual body parts, their whole body was shining with beauty and attractiveness. I felt happy and was mesmerised by them.

The way they talk and the way they behaved was like people in a civilised society. They spoke calmly with a soft voice and flashing smiles. They treated me with much love and respect. They had a very respectful behaviour to each other also. Both males and females were wearing same type of dresses like a gown and plenty of similar jewelleries. Their dresses and jewelleries were full of different valuable stones and were shining all the time. They all had typical golden crowns on their heads topped up with beautiful feathers. They all had golden belts with tiny bells all over and worn across from left shoulder to right waist. When they walked, the bells used to produce a melodious sound.

I was taken to a big hall with golden doors and windows and there were *Banjhankris* seated on the  golden chairs arranged in a U-shape. At the front of the seating arrangement, there was a shining golden throne and the King *Banjhankri* was seated on the throne. They had their own language and the king spoke for a while in their language, which I did not understand. When he finished speaking, two of them took me to the classrooms, library and laboratory hall to observe. Then they took me to the dining hall and served a meal. They had dishes made of earthworms.

Yuck…, I did not want to eat that but how could I dare not to? They all started eating, I had to eat even unwillingly. I thought, they would kill me if I did not eat and therefore, ate a little.

After we had our meal, I was taken to a classroom, where they taught me their first day's lessons. On the first day, they  taught me their language. By the end of day one, I already was able to understand their language. On the second day, I had lessons on their traditions, culture and values and about gods. The third day, they taught me about different evil spirits, how they harm people, what *mantras* to use to make their attack ineffective, how to treat the people attacked by those evil spirits and which different medicinal plants were required together with the *mantras* for the treatment. On day four, they provided me with as same power as they had to travel at their pace and took me with them to the human world to practice fighting against the evil spirits. The fifth day, the last day of my course, they tested my knowledge. At the end of the fifth day, there was a graduation ceremony where they warned me that I should use my acquired knowledge and skill only for the benefit of the people, not to harm them and if I used them to harm the people, all my knowledge and skills would be ineffective then and there and for this, I had to take an oath in the name of the God of shamans. After the graduation ceremony, they took back from me the power of travelling speed they had given to me to travel with them for practice. I was turned back again into an ordinary man as before, except with the knowledges and skills of shamanism and they dropped me back at the spot from where they had picked me up.

The *Bizuwa* had lived in the world of *Banjhankris* for five days. But, when he came back to the human world, he found that five years had passed. His parents were happy to see their missing son back home. He told his parents that he was taken away by *Banjhankris* and he could do the faith healing treatments of the illnesses. Since then, he had treated many patients successfully. At the end, grandma ended storytelling by pronouncing the verse:

To the listeners – gold's garland

To the teller – flower's garland

May this story go direct to the god's land.

While grandma finished the story, I was still lost in the world of *Banjhankris* – their long golden hair, big thick feet, power to travel at flash speed, spiritual powers and that they come time to time to the human world to chase away the evil spirits. Hearing all these stories about them, I remembered myths about *gnomes*, *elves* and *hobbits* I had read about in London. I mentioned about those humans like creatures described in the western myths to grandma and friends. Hearing me, my friends looked at me with great surprise, but grandma reacted simply and said, 'It's the god's creation and may go anywhere in the world.' I found similarities between the *Banjhankris* and *Yetis* and those unusual creatures described in the western literature. It increased my level of interest. I felt like I was being impatient to study the similarities of stories of *Banjhankris*, *Sokpa* or *Yetis* described in the Nepalese folklores and *gnomes*, *elves* and *hobbits* described in the western myths. However, I was happy because I had great stories to share with my friends back in London.

CHAPTER 53

Our returning day and it was nearly time to leave. Our luggage was ready and had already been brought to the front reception room. I was not feeling happy at all to leave grandma, uncle and aunt, especially grandma. She was looking at me and my little sister and her eyes were filling with tears. Seeing her crying, I could not stop myself and my eyes also filled with tears. I ran to her, hugged her tightly and wiped off my tears with her gown. She kissed me a lot on my forehead and cheeks.

'When will you come back again? I have already become old. I may have already died when you come next time.' She said and wiped off her tear with her shawl. I looked at my mom. She was also wiping away her tears. I also almost broke down and started crying but steadied myself and reassured her, 'Grandma, don't even think of dying soon. You will still live for ten fifteen years more. I'll certainly come back in a couple of years. I promise you.' She said 'ok' and kissed my forehead again and extending her both hands, she said, 'Come baby' to my sister. Greta went to her and hugged. Grandma poured all her love on my sister and kissed her several times on her forehead and cheeks.

It was lunch time in the school. My friends came rushing to see me off. I was waiting for them. Grandma did the farewell rituals, fed us yoghurt by a silver cup and spoon, gave us two pieces of banana each and blessed, 'Progress well in your life, have prosperous days ahead and be happy always.'

I had a first-hand feeling then the pain of departing from beloved ones. We proceeded towards the bus park with heavy steps saying bye to them. My friends and my uncle accompanied us to the bus park to see us off.

We caught a bus at two o'clock in the afternoon and reached the airport in the evening. Dad had already booked a hotel room by phone. We went straight to the hotel, dropped our luggage in the room, took a rest for a while and had our dinner.

The road from the village to the airport was not that good. It was a muddy road damaged by the rainwater and some bends that were very scary. I was so tired by the jerking of the bus that I was asleep immediately when I reached my hotel bed.

Mom got me up from the bed early in the morning at six o'clock. We had to check in before seven o'clock for our flight at eight o'clock in the morning. We were in the airport lounge on time.

We were chatting while waiting for the flight. 'How did you find this trip, good?' Dad asked me.

'Not only good dad, it will be one of the most important trips of my life, I think.' I replied.

Meanwhile, the siren of the airport tower sounded. It was a signal that the plane was approaching. I went close to the window and looked through it. I saw a plane coming from the south of the *Arun* valley flying in between the two mountains over *Arun* river. From a distance, it looked like an eagle flying. It gradually came closer and became bigger. I took photographs of the plane landing.

The door of the plane opened. Passengers got off and moved towards the luggage claim area. There were two pilots and they also came out of the cockpit. Passengers were called for boarding and we also stood in the queue. The pilots had come out of the plane for a cigarette. They came and stood a bit away from us. What a pleasant coincidence! Perhaps, luck was in my favour. The captain of the plane was my dad's classmate in the school, and he was from the same village.

When he saw my dad in the queue, he came close to us. He shook hand with dad and said, 'Om, when did you come home? I did not know you were coming. If known, we could have enjoyed one evening together. Please let me know next time, ok?'

'It would really be great if we could have spent couple of hours together. But what you know Suresh, I have been out of contact. I do not have your contact details, telephone or email. Let's exchange it now.' Dad answered him and they exchanged their telephone numbers and email addresses. Dad introduced mom, me and Greta to him.

'This is the first time my children have come home. My son has enjoyed very much the beauty of the village and the area. Suresh, will you be able to take go round the valley while flying back to Kathmandu? He will have a chance to have a good aerial view of the natural beauty as well.' Dad did not forget to request him.

'Sure, I'll do it for our boy', the captain agreed and told me putting his hand on my shoulder, 'Dear, take your seat in the plane at the window on right side. Today, the weather is clear, and you will have a very nice view of the mountain as well.'

It was as if my luck was soaring. I had supportive and positive opportunities one after another. I shook my head with pleasure and said, 'thank you.'

Then we boarded the plane and I took a seat on right row by the window. After all passengers boarded, the door of the plane closed. The pilots got into the cockpit, got everything ready to fly and started the engine. I got my camera ready to take photographs from the plane. The plane took off and made a round of the area. Amazing! What a natural beauty! I viewed everything and saved them in my heart. The plane had already gained its height when it made a full round of the area and flew west for Kathmandu. I viewed those majestic scenes of the white Himalayan range to the north, the peaks of the mountains, valleys and the beauty wrapped by a shawl of greenery.

This was my last chance to have a direct view of such beautiful scenes in this trip. I knew that I would soon have only memories of such beautiful scenes. So, I kept my camera ready and took many photos from the plane.

CHAPTER 54

I was back in London and at my school. As planned, the photo exhibition was organised successfully in my school. I was happy because my photo exhibition had been so successful. Two things emerged out of the photo exhibition which may impact my future.

First, the fund from the exhibition for my school support project has been raised three times more than my target of two thousand five hundred pounds. To make this amount, not only from the sales of the items in the exhibition but also the visitors made generous donations on the spot. Every visitor was saying the same version, 'Robin, not only two schools of your village but support other schools in the same conditions as long as you can.' This caused a new motivation within me. Not only me, Philip, Ade, Chris and many other friends of mine, since they heard from me about my visit, were also equally motivated to prepare for the exhibition and extended their helping hands. From the exhibition, more than eight thousand pounds were raised and I could support an additional seven schools from the surrounding villages. After that encouraging event, we formed a team and have been actively raising money for charity.

Second, seeing the photographs of stunning natural beauty and hearing interesting travel memoirs and folklores, my friends expressed their interest to visit Nepal. Philip, Ade and Chris even planned to go to Nepal with me after we complete our study. We decided to wait until we finish school and then go and live in Nepal for a month or more, for sightseeing, adventure and to understand the people and their traditions.

All four of us, Philip, Ade, Chris and I, have the same thoughts in our mind, we imagine our future adventures and look forward to seeing a piece of heaven on earth, a paradise, the *Shangri-la,* as James Hilton has described the *Sangri-la* in his work *Lost Horizon.*

Printed in Great Britain
by Amazon

80317634R00180